REBORN

DAN MAYER

Black Rose Writing | Texas

The final approval for this literary material is granted by the author.

First printing

This is a work of fiction. Names, characters, businesses, places, events and incidents are either the products of the author's imagination or used in a fictitious manner. Any resemblance to actual persons, living or dead, or actual events is purely coincidental.

ISBN: 978-1-68433-132-1
PUBLISHED BY BLACK ROSE WRITING
www.blackrosewriting.com

Printed in the United States of America
Suggested Retail Price (SRP) $17.95

Reborn is printed in Book Antiqua

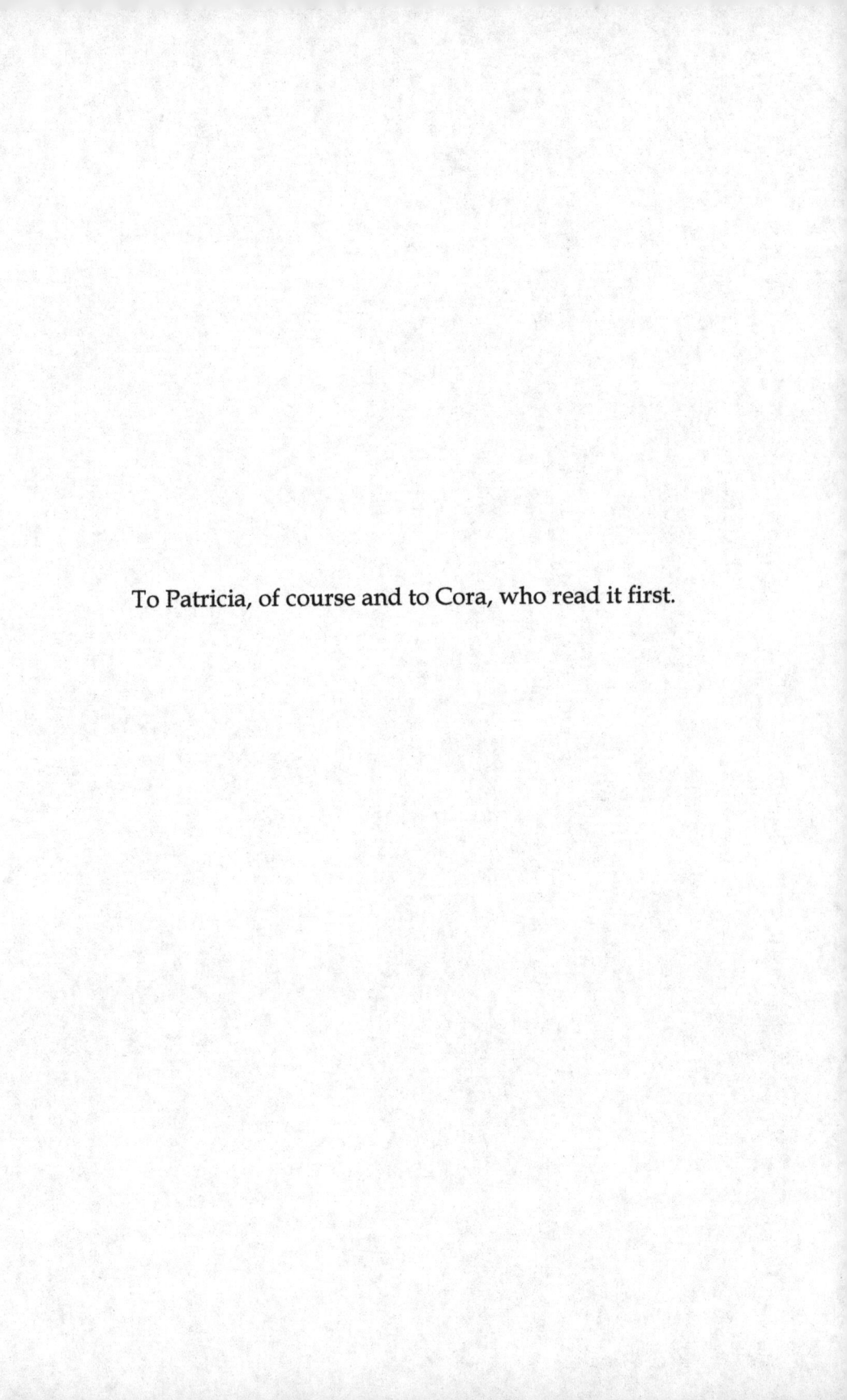

To Patricia, of course and to Cora, who read it first.

REBORN

REBORN

CHAPTER ONE

"If you don't mind me saying; you look like a man that's down on his luck," the stranger said.

Walt jumped. He thought that he was alone, and the sound from behind him in the darkness, startled him.

"Who's there?"

"Hi there, my name is Joshua," he said, extending his hand, as he walked out from the shadows.

"I'm sorry. I didn't mean to startle you. Please accept my apologies."

"It's alright. Don't worry about it," Walt said, extending his hand to shake Joshua's.

Joshua was a slender black man that stood about six feet two inches tall. He was wearing a tailored suit and he had an air of dignity about him. Hardly the type of person you would expect to meet in a dark, back alley. His hair was cut short and it was greying at his temples; but it was his smile that really set him apart.

They say that the eyes are the windows to the soul, but someone's smile can tell you everything you need to know about them. It's nearly impossible to fake a warm and genuine smile. Joshua had a smile that made you smile back.

A blue spark of electricity jumped from Joshua's hand to Walt's, causing Walt to pull his hand back for a second. When he did finally shake Joshua's hand, it was like shaking the hand of his Grandfather. He had a firm handshake, but not too firm. His hand seemed to melt into Joshua's and he felt a little embarrassed that his hand lingered there, longer than it probably should have.

"What brings you to my little slice of heaven?" Walt said, lifting his arm and making a sweeping gesture from one side of the alley to the other.

"I'm a traveler. I travel the world and every new country or new town that I visit, I like to see all of it. I'm not talking about the tourist traps or just the beautiful places. No, I'm talking about seeing every facet of the places I visit. In doing so, I meet people that the ordinary traveler would never meet. Sometimes, people that they wouldn't want to meet. I get to see the real-life struggles, that most people never see, never get to experience. These are the places that I get to meet some genuinely surprising individuals," Joshua said, flashing his enormous, warm smile.

"Whatever floats your boat," Walt said sarcastically.

"So, if you have a minute. I'd like to talk to you. If that's okay? I'd like to get your take on this town. You know, from a local person's point of view."

"Sure. I got nothing but time to kill. You a reporter or something?"

"No, I'm not a reporter. What I do is not important right now. I may get to that later. We'll see how the conversation goes and then we'll take it from there," Joshua said.

"Whatever. Like I said before, I got nothing but time on my hands and I could use the company."

"That's good, very good," Joshua said, and then sat down on the ground, facing him.

Walt would normally be a little weirded out by a guy that wanted to sit in an alley and talk at three in the morning, especially when the guy was wearing a tailored suit. This guy was different though. He couldn't put his finger on it, but he just knew, that this guy would be alright. Maybe it was his warm smile or his soothing voice, but whatever it was, it made him feel at ease. Actually, he reminded him of his Grandma. She always had a warm smile for him and a kind word, but that seemed like a hundred years ago, now. A hundred years, countless foster homes and a couple incarcerations since.

"So, what's your deal man? We're sitting in a back alley in the middle of the night and you're wearing a suit like that, what gives? Hell, most people around here would kill you just to take your shoes, not to mention your suit and that briefcase of yours."

"I'm not worried," he simply said.

"Well, you should be. You have nothing to worry about from me. I'm just saying."

"I know. I can read people very well, that's what I do. I know all about you."

"You don't know shit, man. Look at you, with your fancy clothes. You're probably wearing a Rolex under there. You think you know me. You don't know nothing about me or the shit I've been through. You think you do, but until you've been through it; you don't know shit. You're lucky you're still alive. You pull this shit in some parts of town or with the wrong people, and you wouldn't be so smug. You'd be dead," Walt said, loudly.

"I'm sorry. I think we got off on the wrong foot. I'm not trying to diminish the struggles that you have been through or the hardships that you have endured. I just meant that I've been around enough to have seen it all, you know?" Joshua said.

"It's all good. No worries man. You are right about one thing. I wouldn't be sleeping in this fuckin' alley if my life was going according to plan. You don't have to be a psychic to figure that much out. So, what's your deal? You don't look like a guy that's down on his luck. Looks like life is treating you alright. So, why are you sitting in an alley with a bum at three in the morning? I got nothing but time man. Come on, give it to me straight. What's your deal man?" Walt asked.

"Okay, you asked for it," Joshua said, laughing a little.

He reached inside his jacket and pulled out a pipe, stuffed a couple of pinches of tobacco into it, lit it, and then took a short haul on the end of it. He sat for a moment with his eyes closed, clearly enjoying it. Then he opened his eyes and looked at Walt again.

"I forgot how good that is. I really missed it. I just didn't know how much until this very moment. It's funny you know? Of all the things in this world and that's the one thing that I missed the most."

"You just get out or something?" Walt asked.

"No, no, that's not it. Never been to jail," Joshua said, laughing and then continuing.

"So, we have some time to kill. Did you want me to tell you my story, or would you like to tell your story? Are you in the mood to talk or listen, is my question?" Joshua asked.

"You know what. What the Hell, I'll play along. I'll tell you my story, but it's not gonna be a happy one, with no happy ending."

Joshua motioned for Walt to continue, and so he began to recount his story up until now.

"I didn't always call this alley home you know. Actually, it's only been four days since I've been out on my ear. Couldn't pay the rent and so my landlord kicked me out. I had some offers to make a few quick bucks but I decided come Hell or high water, that I was going to go it straight this time. I'm done with doing time. I figure, as long as I'm on the outside, I have a chance of things turning around and going my way, you know? Anyway, when I was a kid everything was as it should be. I had great parents and we lived in a nice place in a middle-class neighbourhood, just west of here. My Mom was a stay at home Mom and my Dad worked for an automotive supplier in Drummondsville. They put me in soccer in the summer and I went rabbit hunting with my Dad in the winter. I was the poster child for the happy, middle-class lifestyle. In the blink of an eye, that all changed, one rainy August night when I was twelve. My parents went to a party at Sharon's house. Sharon was my Mom's best friend and so I spent a lot of time there as a kid, while my parents visited. I was perfectly okay with that. Sharon and Bill have a daughter named Elise. We played together the whole time we were growing up. Elise was a year older than me, and as she got older I couldn't help but notice when she started to mature, if you know what I mean. Anyway, we went from playing board games, to playing house. I was younger so nothing really happened. She let me kiss her and play with her breasts that kind of stuff. I still see her once in a while, but she won't give me the time of day any more. Too bad, because she turned out to be a real looker. It's just that we kind of took different paths, you know? She took the normal route of going to college and then getting a good job and I went to jail instead. Okay, so anyway, back to my parents. They were on their way home from Sharon's and my Dad was driving. He wasn't drunk or anything. My Dad never drank really. He'd have a beer sometimes, but he never really drank on a regular basis. No one really knows what happened. Maybe a deer ran out in front of them or something; who knows. All I know for sure is that he lost control of the car and hit a tree. Mom was thrown from the car and died instantly. Dad hung around for a few days. I remember going to the hospital with my Grandma, to visit him. He never did regain consciousness and he died three days later. Then it was just my Grandma and me. She was a sweetheart. She helped me through that tough time in my life and look how I repaid her. After she died two years later, I was on my own. I was fourteen and I was mad as Hell at the world. My parents were gone and now my Grandma was too. I didn't have any family here so I ended up a ward of the state. I was a miserable son of a bitch. No foster home I went to, had a chance in Hell of straightening me out. I hated everyone and everything, and on top of that, I was at the age that I knew everything and nobody could tell me anything. I skipped school all the time and I got in a lot of fights. Harmless stuff really. Not much different, then a lot of kids. I went from one foster home to another. I think I went through six in total before I was done. And you know, they weren't bad people. None of them did anything to me or treated me poorly, really. I hear all kinds of horror stories about kids being abused or molested. I had nothing like that happen to me. My problem was me, not them. I had been hanging around with an older crowd and started drinking a bit. I think they thought it was kind of fun to get the young kid drunk. I was probably more of a novelty to them, but at the time I didn't realize it. I just knew, that I was getting drunk for free and I thought they were my friends.

One day I went to a bush lot party just out of town. A few people had planned on staying there overnight and so they pitched tents. There was a big bon fire and the tunes were provided by Larry Benn's Chevy. He had spent some serious coin on his sound system and he was happy to show it off any chance he got. Anyway, on this particular night, Elise was there with a bunch of her friends and she was clearly drunk. Abe Warren, the asshole captain of the high school football team was there with a bunch of his asshole friends. They were picking on some of the nerds that were there, and then Abe set his sights on Elise. He took her into one of the tents. She protested a bit but he was persistent and so she eventually followed him. His buddies stayed in front of the tent for a while to guard the entrance, I suppose. Eventually they got bored and moved off. I moved closer to the tent so that I could hear what was going on over the loud music. I wasn't creeping her, I just had a bad feeling about what Abe would do. When I got close, I could hear that Elise was still telling him no, and he was still telling her that it would be fine. This continued back and forth a couple of times and then I could tell that she was crying. I'd had enough and so I ripped open the zipper of the tent and looked inside. Abe jerked his head around and yelled at me to get out. I barely heard him, my focus was on Elise. She was lying on a sleeping bag in the middle of the tent and Abe was on top of her. Her pants were down around her knees and Abe's pants were unbuttoned and his fly was open. Elise was crying and there were dark streaks down her cheeks where her mascara had run from her tears. One look at what was happening and I completely lost control. I threw Abe off Elise and then jumped on top of him. Under normal circumstances, Abe probably would have gotten the best of me, but I had the element of surprise and boy was he surprised. I was on top of him in a flash and I rained punches down on his face until I was so completely out of breath that I nearly passed out. When I came to my senses, I looked down and Abe was a bloody mess. His nose was broken in several spots, his left eye was swollen shut and his bottom lip was split wide open. He was unconscious and Elise was screaming at the top of her lungs for me to stop, even though I already had. I didn't feel any remorse for what I had done, because I knew that I had saved Elise from being raped.

Nothing happened to Abe, but I was convicted of aggravated assault and I was tried as an adult. You know how small towns are.

The captain of the football team is king of the land and is untouchable, so they threw the book at me.

That was the beginning of my path to where I am right now. I spent two years less a day in the clink. I was in with the general population and I was only sixteen. So, you can probably fill in the blanks. Let's just say I learned a lot of new skills on the inside, that I would rather not have learned. Anyway, when I got out, I was mad at the world and I got into a few more scrapes with the law, because of my temper. Just a couple of fights, nothing serious but I broke parole, so it was back inside for me. Then when I got out again, I kinda learned from those mistakes and I tried to go it straight, but I couldn't find a job and so a friend of mine hooked me up with a sure-fire thing. Like there is such a thing. I got caught stealing from some rich guy's safe. He had cameras on top of cameras watching the place. I should have known better, but I believed my buddy and look where it got me; back on the inside, that's where it got me. My buddy got his share and I got fucked. I could have served less time if I ratted him out but I didn't. I got out a few weeks ago and tried to find him but, poof, vanished. I've been trying to figure out my next move, but nothing has come to me yet. I tried getting work but no one will touch me. I might try moving to another town. It can't hurt. I know one thing, and that's no matter what happens, I'm not going back inside. I'm done with that game. I'll starve to death first," Walt said, finishing his story, and then sat looking across the alley to where Joshua was sitting, smoking his pipe.

"You're right about one thing, no happy ending there. Not yet anyway. That part of your story is over and there's no changing it, but you still have the chance for a happy life. Let me tell you my story and then you can decide what you want to do. Does that seem fair?" Joshua asked.

"Whatever man. I'll hear your story. You listened to my hard luck story. The least I can do is to listen to yours. I have a feeling that yours is going to be a lot happier than mine," Walt said.

"Why do you say that?"

"Look at the way you're dressed. You can't tell me that things have worked out all that bad for you," Walt scoffed.

"It's not the clothes that make a man. I'm sure you've heard that expression. It's not money for that matter, either. When you were younger and your parents were alive, what do you remember most from that time? Was it the fact that your Dad had a good job, that you lived in a nice house and that your parents drove a nice car? When they died and you went to live with your Grandma; what do you remember most about that time? Never mind, I know the answers to those questions. It's the love that they showed you. Isn't that right?" Joshua asked.

"Yeah, I guess you're right. They were always there for me. If my parents and my Grandma had never died, then things would have turned out completely different for me."

"Right! We all have many paths we can go down. We think it's the circumstances in our lives that lead us to where we are today, but that's not true. It's the choices that we make along the way. Now let me tell you my story and then I think you may have a few questions for me," Joshua said, smiling coyly.

"I was born in the south. My parents were slaves and so upon birth, I was also a slave," Joshua started.

"Let me stop you right there. Unless you're well over a hundred years old or my math is completely wrong, then you're either a liar or you're just telling a story. I told you my story and I'd appreciate it, if you would tell me yours," Walt said, interrupting him.

"Okay, okay. I don't need to go back that far anyway. I'll give you as true an account as I can recall.

"My early years were a struggle but when I got older I thought that I was really living the life. I was living in a nice house, I had a nice car and I was making lots of money. I had moved to Boston and I became an accountant. I was doing the books for some very influential people. I thought I had made it. I couldn't have been further from the truth. They owned me. It was as though I were a slave."

"Now I understand the reference to being a slave," Walt interjected.

"Sorry, please continue. I'll try not to interrupt again."

"I tried to believe that I was happy. How could I not be? I had everything that I wanted. Ahh, but I didn't have anything. Some very old clichés are the best, because they are so true. Money can't buy happiness, is one of them. I had to jump when my clients said to and I had to work long hours, sometimes when I didn't want to. My life was not my own. Sure, I had a lot of money, but I didn't have the time to enjoy it, or someone to enjoy it with.

When I first moved to Boston, I met a beautiful girl name Maggie. She was white and had long blonde hair. Well, back then, a white girl dating a black man was not an everyday occurrence, and it certainly wasn't accepted. We didn't give a hoot what anyone thought. We were in love and that was all that mattered. That should have been enough, but I had to prove to her and to me that they were all wrong. I had to prove that I deserved to be with Maggie. She couldn't care a less about a fancy car or a fancy house but I was determined to give her the best of everything. All she wanted was me, but I was too stupid to see it. I worked long hours and spent less and less time with her. I kept chasing something that wasn't there. What I should have realized was, what I truly wanted was right in front of me. What's that expression? You don't know what you got 'till it's gone. Well, one day I came home from another long night at the office. I was exhausted and all I wanted to do was curl up on the sofa with Maggie and have a glass of wine and talk. The sofa was gone and so was Maggie. I tried to contact her but she wouldn't return my calls. She went to stay with her sister. I tried to talk to her there but her sister called the cops on me. I tried a couple more times over the next few weeks but she wouldn't talk to me. Now I could see what I couldn't before, when Maggie was still around, that she was the most important thing in my life and that without her, nothing else mattered. I wrote her countless letters, apologizing for my behaviour and begging for her to forgive me. She never responded, but the silence spoke volumes. She had moved on. Everything would have been okay I guess, if my eyes hadn't been opened to the fact, that there is more to life than money. I could have been completely content to work like a madman and I would have become extremely wealthy. But, my eyes were now fully open; now that it was too late. I became extremely depressed. I could hardly think, let alone work. When I did think, it was only about Maggie and how much I had screwed up. I wanted to kill myself but I was too much of a coward to do it. So, I did it slowly. I had lots of money at my disposal and I was no longer saving for a rainy day, so the sky was the limit. I had all kinds of new friends to party with and all sorts of beautiful women to sleep with. I spent seventy thousand dollars in five months and I was more miserable than when I started. I continued to drink and do drugs. My clients had dropped me long ago and so I had no new money coming in. Every time I thought that I had hit rock bottom, the bottom was pulled out from beneath me. I went tumbling further down into an abyss that I had no way of pulling myself free from.

It was Christmas morning, and I sat in front of an undecorated tree in my living room. There were no presents under it, no parties to attend and no loved ones. I had finally and completely hit rock bottom and I no longer wanted to crawl out of the hole that I was in. All I wanted, was for it to end. I went to the bedroom and got my thirty-eight from my sock drawer, carried it out into the living room and sat down on the sofa. I didn't spend hours contemplating where I went wrong, or thinking of reasons why I should live. I lifted the gun, put the barrel against my temple and pulled the trigger."

CHAPTER TWO

If he didn't before, he sure had Walt's undivided attention now.

"Holy shit! What happened? How'd you live through that? You forget to put one in the chamber? You forgot, didn't you? Yeah, there's no other explanation."

"No, I didn't forget to put one in the chamber," Joshua said, evenly.

"Bullshit man! You wouldn't be sittin' here if you had."

Joshua didn't respond. He just turned his head sideways so that Walt could see the small round scar on his temple. The moon shone enough light into the alley, that he could just make it out. Then he turned his head the other way. There was a spider web of scars that spread out from his other temple, about two inches in diameter.

Walt acted as though he had seen a ghost. He tried to push himself away from Joshua but the wall held his back in place.

"What the fuck man! How'd you live through that! No one could live through that!" Walt yelled.

"Okay. Calm down and I'll explain. Take a couple deep breaths, relax. That's it," Joshua said, in the most soothing voice that he could muster.

Walt took a deep breath and let it out slowly and then did it again. He repeated it one more time and it had the desired effect, that Joshua had hoped for. He was calmer now, but that had as much to do with Joshua's soothing voice, as it did with his breathing. He had questions though. No doubt about it, he had questions.

Joshua could see it written all over his face. Walt had a lot of questions. They always did.

"I'm going to ask you to remain calm. Can you do that? If you need to, just take a few more deep breaths. It'll help you to relax," Joshua said.

"I'm fine. Just get on with your story," Walt snapped back at him.

"Okay. I backed off from my story earlier because I could see that we were getting off on the wrong foot. Everything I have told you is the absolute truth. I was born a slave in the south and I died Christmas day forty-nine years ago, from a self-inflicted gun-shot wound to the head.

Walt took a deep breath to calm himself, but his eyes were as wide as saucers. Joshua had his undivided attention.

"I'm not really sure why I was chosen for this job. All I know is that I was. Like I said before, I travel all over the world looking for people, just like you. When I said that I knew all about you, I wasn't speaking metaphorically. I really do know all about you. I was sent to talk to you. At the end of the day, I still get to decide whether to proceed or not. That's why I like to talk to people first. I like to get a feel for what they're like. I want to know what makes them tick. I want to see behind their rough exteriors, past the wall that they have built to protect themselves. Some people don't give me the time of day and that's fine. I just move on to the next person on the list. I like you Walt. You didn't just brush me off. You sat with a complete stranger in a back alley and told me your life story, and as far as I could tell, you were completely honest with me. As I said before; circumstances don't make us who we are. It is the choices that we make during or afterwards that determines which direction we will take in life. What would we do differently, if we were given a second chance? Now, your case is a little different than most. Your Mom and Dad dying and then your Grandma as well, were certainly nothing you could change. The choices that you made afterward could have changed, certainly. It seems to me, that when you saved Elise from being raped at the party that that was the pivotal part in your story. Let me ask you a question. If you were given a second chance, knowing that saving Elise would end with you serving time and then bringing you to this point in your life; would you do it?"

There was no hesitation. Walt didn't need time to think about his answer. There was no way that he would allow Elise to be harmed in any way. He had always loved Elise and even though they had grown apart over the years, he would always look out for her.

"In a heartbeat. There's no way that I would stand by and do nothing, knowing that someone was about to be harmed, especially Elise."

"Good answer. Right answer," Joshua said, smiling and then chuckling a little.

"Who are you anyway? Are you an angel or something?" Walt asked.

"Oh, I'm something alright. I'll get to that in good time. Let me finish saying what I was about to say. I know that this is a lot to take in, but we have nowhere else to be, right? Now, when you saved Elise, it set into motion a whole series of events that stemmed from your decision to beat Abe to a pulp. Let's go back a bit, shall we? After the death of your parents and then your Grandma, you were very bitter. All the decisions that you made at that time may have been different if you weren't mad at the world," Joshua said, and stood waiting patiently for Walt's response.

"I know what you're saying. Everything that we do in our life has consequences and as trivial as some decisions might seem to be at the time, they all have an impact in our life. Is that right?"

"Exactly! Now, whether you decide to put sugar in your coffee or not, for example, might not be a life altering decision, but it does affect your life in some small way. You being mad at the world certainly did have a dramatic effect on your life. I wish I could say that I could go back and save your parents and that it would make everything okay, but I can't. I can help guide you and I can send you back, but the rest is up to you."

"What do you mean, you can send me back?" Walt asked.

"Okay. Let me tell you what my function here is, and then I'll go over the ground rules and if you're still interested, we can talk more about what I can do for you. You asked me before if I was an angel. I don't know what I am. I know I bleed like everyone else. I know that I died on that Christmas day, so long ago, but that I'm alive now. I know that I haven't aged a day since. Sometimes, depending on how the case goes, I feel younger than ever. I know that I was given a job to do and that I take that job very seriously. You're probably wondering who gave me this job. Well, I didn't sit down with God and discuss what my responsibilities were, if that's what you're thinking. When I awoke after my run in with my .38, I just knew. I don't know how to explain it. It's kind of like someone downloaded a user manual into my brain, you know? I only know what I know and that certainly isn't everything.

I can send you back to a time before everything began to unravel for you. Why some people are given this chance while others aren't, I can't say, because I just don't know. I still can't figure out how I got here. If you decide to go back, you'll have to live it all over again; your parents' deaths and then your Grandma's death. The good news is that you can change things in your life that led you down the path to jail. You wouldn't be allowed to tell anyone about our little arrangement and just as a safe guard, you wouldn't be able to if you tried. If you screw it up again, you would have another chance to get it right after that. It's a very generous offer when you think about it. A word of caution though. I've seen it go much worse for some people, but the majority of people get it right the second time around. To be honest, I wish I would have been given this offer. I would have jumped at it in a heartbeat. I would have spent more time at home and been a better husband to Maggie. Anyway, any questions?" Joshua asked, when he had finished.

"Surprisingly, I don't have a lot of questions. I'm sure I'll have a ton of them later, when it's too late," Walt said.

"I'll be around to guide you through the process. So, if any questions come up, I'll be happy to answer them along the way," Joshua said.

"Okay, so how does this work? How do you send me back?" Walt asked.

"I don't, you do," Joshua said, producing his .38 from his pocket.

"Are you shittin' me? You think I'm going to kill myself!" Walt said, loudly.

"You can't go back if you're still here. Listen, everything will be fine, you'll see," Joshua said in his beautiful, soothing voice.

Walt was so reassured by Joshua's voice that he barely hesitated. He grabbed the gun from Joshua's outstretched hand and a blue spark jumped to his fingertips. He stopped to think of the last few years of his life. His parents' deaths and then his Grandma's. He thought of Elise and how sad he was that they had drifted apart. He knew that it was all his fault that they had. He desperately wanted a second chance to make it right with her. He wanted a second chance period. How many people would ever get the chance that he was being given. Fuck it! What did he have to lose!

"How will I find you?" Walt asked.

"No worries. I'll find you," Joshua said.

"Okay. I guess I'll see you on the other side then."

Walt took a couple of deep breaths; in through his nose and then let them out slowly through his mouth. He was beginning to sweat and his mouth was going dry but he knew that if he didn't do it soon, that he would lose his nerve. It would be hard to go through the deaths of his parents and his Grandma again, but he would also be getting a new lease on life. This time he was going to do it right. This time he wasn't going to push Elise away.

He lifted the .38 to his temple, took a deep breath and pulled the trigger.

CHAPTER THREE

Walt lie in bed with his eyes closed. It was Saturday morning and he could hear his parents getting breakfast ready. He could smell sausages and maple syrup. He lie there thinking about his dream. It was the longest, most complex dream in his entire life. He heard it said once, that the average dream is only thirty-four seconds. Surely this dream must have been much longer. It seemed as though he had been dreaming from the time that he fell asleep, until the time that he awoke.

"Breakfast is ready," his Mom called, from the kitchen.

Walt was hungry, but he was still busy going over the dream in his mind, and he wasn't ready to get up just yet.

"Are you going to stay in bed all day?" his Dad called.

"Be out in a minute."

He couldn't believe how real it had seemed. He didn't know what he would do without his Mom and Dad or Grandma for that matter. He shivered at the thought. He tried to shake free from his terrible dream, but it wouldn't let go of him.

He went to the bathroom to go pee and brush his teeth. Maybe splashing water on his face would be just the thing to shake the dream from his mind. He ran the water until it was as cold as it would get, then filled his cupped hands and splashed it on his cheeks and fore head. The cold water was refreshing, and he repeated the process, enjoying the sensation for a second time. The dream was beginning to fade to the back of his mind, but before it did; a thought came to mind that scared him again. He pushed back his hair with his hand and turned his face to the side so that he could see his temple.

Nothing. He exhaled and chuckled a little. What did he expect to find? It was just a dream, but a very real dream all the same. Just to be sure though, he pushed back the hair from the other side to reveal his other temple. Nothing. He breathed a sigh of relief and went out into the kitchen.

"It lives. Thought you were going to stay in bed all day," his Dad said.

"I just couldn't seem to get moving. I had a strange dream and I couldn't shake it."

"Anything you want to talk about?" his Mom asked.

"Not really. It's already starting to fade. I can only remember the highlights, so it wouldn't make sense," Walt said.

That was only partly true. He had forgotten a bit, but most of the dream still seemed as real as when he first woke up. The soothing sound of Joshua's voice and all the events of his dream, seemed to have actually happened. They felt like real memories. It was so detailed and so lengthy, that he was having a hard time just letting go of it.

"Well, okay. Eat your breakfast before it gets cold," his Dad said.

"Remember; Grandma's coming over tonight. Your Dad and I have to go to Sharon and Bill's for supper. We're celebrating her new promotion," his Mom said.

"Oh yeah."

Hairs stood up on the back of his head and neck. A shiver ran through him. A sense of dread and foreboding filled him.

"Do you have to go?" Walt asked.

"Of course, we do. This is a big deal for Sharon and Dave. I wouldn't miss it for the world. Why? What's gotten into you? I thought you loved hanging out with G-ma," his Mom asked.

"I do. It's just that my dream has me a little spooked, that's all."

"Why? What happened in your dream that has you so flustered?" his Dad asked.

"Honestly? You guys died in a car accident."

"Wow. Okay, now I see what has you all worked up. Listen, it was just a dream, all right? Your Mom and I aren't going to die. I'll be

23

extra careful driving tonight. Okay?"

"Okay. I know it might seem silly, but be careful, please," Walt said.

"We will," they said, and hugged him tightly.

Walt smiled at them and put on a brave face, but until this night was behind them, he was going to worry.

He finished breakfast and helped his mom with the dishes while his Dad went out to tinker in the garage. Afterwards, he continued as best he could, as though it was just another ordinary Saturday. He watched cartoons and then read a book for a while. No matter what he did, he just couldn't shake the dream. He decided he needed to go and talk to someone about it. There was only one person that he ever really shared his true thoughts with and that was Elise. If he knew her, she would be in her bedroom reading a book as well, so he didn't bother to call, he just rode his bike over.

"Going to Elise's," he said to his Dad, as he grabbed his bike.

"Okay, have fun. Don't be all day. Grandma's coming at three and it's supposed to rain later."

"Okay."

There was that terrible sense of foreboding again. It was raining in his dream, the night that his parents died. He looked up at the clear blue sky and it set his mind at ease, a little. The weatherman was never right. No way it was going to rain. There was barely a cloud in the sky.

He took his time getting to Elise's. Not surprisingly, he had other things on his mind at the moment. He arrived at Elise's but he couldn't recall how he had gotten there. His mind had been on autopilot. The only thing he remembered was nearly being taken out by a guy driving a purple Ford pick-up, when he coasted through a stop sign.

"Hi Walt. How's it going? Elise is in her bedroom reading. Just go on in," Elise's Mom said cheerfully.

"Hi Mrs. Reid. I'm doing alright, and you?"

"Wonderful. Thanks for asking."

Walt found Elise in her bedroom reading, just as Sharon said she would be. Really, where else would she be on a Saturday morning. Elise was such a bookworm. She read more than Walt did and that was saying something, because he read a ton.

"What ya reading?"

"It's called The Suffering. It's about a guy that gets off on bullying people and then later, hurting people and animals."

"Oh, sounds great."

"No, it is. You'd have to read it, I guess. I like the guy. I feel sorry for him. He's really a good guy," she said.

"Sounds like it."

"It's not like that! I'll let you read it when I'm finished. I only have a couple of chapters to go. I started it last night and I can't put it down. What brings you by? I thought that you would be at home reading or watching cartoons."

"This is going to sound silly, but I had the craziest, most incredibly real dream in my life and I just can't seem to shake it. I thought that if I told you about it, then maybe it would help."

Elise snapped her book shut and sat up straight in her bed.

"I'm all ears. Sounds intriguing."

He told her about his dream. He told her about Joshua, about how he was older and that they had drifted apart and his parents and his Grandma were dead. He told her that they had died on their way back from her place; which happened to be tonight.

"Wow! No wonder you're freaked out. You know how I know it was just a crazy dream though?" she said, giggling.

"Because I don't think that we could ever drift apart. You're stuck with me forever," she said, leaning forward and kissing him.

Walt kissed her back and then hugged her.

"I know it's crazy, but do you think you can come over tonight to keep me company anyway?" Walt asked.

"I'm sure my parents won't care. That way I won't be around for their little party."

"That would be great… You think I'm being a big baby?"

"No way! If I had a dream like that, it would freak me out too; but it'll be fine. You'll see."

Walt and Elise talked for a while, and his feeling of unease slowly faded. She had a way about her that always made him feel comfortable. She was right. He couldn't imagine that they would ever grow apart.

"What do you say we go down to the river for a while?" Walt asked.

"That's a good idea. Let me grab my bathing suit and I'll be right back."

"Okay. We'll have to swing by my place on the way so that I can change first," he said.

Elise was gone a minute and then returned, wearing an orange bikini. She threw a cover over top, and she was ready to go. They stopped by at his house so he could change and then they were off to the river. They spent a lot of time there, especially this summer. It was hot nearly every day and it very rarely rained. They enjoyed the afternoon swimming in the large pool in the bend of the river and then catching crayfish in the shallows. Walt had forgotten all about his silly dream. The bright blue sky was slowly becoming more and more overcast as the day passed. Wisps of white clouds floated lazily by, the wind brought with it darker grey ones and eventually they were replaced with dark black clouds. Walt and Elise were having so much fun that they didn't even notice, until it started to rain. Walt saw the first few rain drops falling on the smooth water of the pool. He looked up, seeing for the first time, that the clear blue sky had been replaced by black clouds, full of rain.

"It's raining!" Walt said, sounding scared.

"So what, silly. We're already wet," Elise said, starting to laugh, but the smile quickly faded from her face.

She could see the worried look on Walt's face and she understood. In his dream, it had been raining on the day that his parents were killed.

"Come on Walt. It was just a dream. You know that, right?"

"I know that, but another part of me just can't shake this bad feeling I have."

Elise came over to him, put her arms around his neck and rested her forehead on his.

"It'll be fine. You guys don't live far from our house; besides, your Dad is as careful a driver as there is."

"I know you're right. It's just…" Walt said.

"Come on. Let's go. I'm going to run back home and get some fresh clothes. I'll see if my Mom will give me some money for pizza," she said, spinning away from him and running up the slope to where their bikes were lying in the gravel, at the top of the hill.

"Sounds good. I'll see if my Mom will give me some money too."

"Okay, I'll meet you at your house in half an hour," Elise said.

Walt was at his house a few minutes later. He went into the laundry room and grabbed a towel to dry himself off. He got changed and went to find his Mom.

"Hey, Elise is going to come over while you guys go to her house later, if that's okay."

"That's fine honey."

"I was wondering if I could get some money for pizza."

"Sure, but remember Grandma is coming over, so I want you to order in. Besides, it looks like we're in for a good storm and I don't want you out in it."

I don't want you out in it either, Walt thought, but said nothing.

Grandma arrived shortly after and Elise got there not long after that. His Mom and Dad started to get ready to go and Walt was getting more nervous as time passed. The wind had increased measurably and the driving rain was quite loud against the side of the house and the tin roof. Elise was beside him. She grabbed his hand and squeezed it for reassurance.

"You'll look back on this and laugh. You'll see," she whispered in his ear.

Walt's parents left and they ordered pizza. Elise and Walt shared one, because his Grandma liked hers with just pepperoni and cheese and they liked theirs with the works. Pizza was one of his favourite foods in the whole world and normally he would be savouring every bite. Not tonight however. He spent the entire night waiting for the other shoe to drop. He knew it was crazy and Elise did her best to reassure him, but until his parents were safe at home, he would continue to worry. Grandma fell asleep shortly after dinner and so Walt and Elise went into his room and watched videos on you-tube. The videos distracted him a bit, but he couldn't make it more than a few minutes without checking the display on his alarm clock that sat on his nightstand.

The display at the present read 10 o'clock and he had no real idea of when he expected their return. He wished now that he would have thought to ask them.

"Don't worry so much. You never were good at hiding anything. You're like an open book; it's written all over your face," Elise said.

"I know. I'm sorry I'm such a downer tonight. Just let me get through tonight and then I'll feel much better."

Elise set the laptop aside, laid down beside him and put her head on his chest. Walt wrapped his arms around her and held her tightly. They lie that way, with neither of them talking, enjoying the comfort of just being together, until Elise finally broke the silence.

"I told you. Nothing could ever tear us apart. Together forever," she said.

Walt sighed and squeezed her for a second. For the first time in hours he was able to relax.

CHAPTER FOUR

"That was nice. I'm so happy for Sharon. She really deserves everything that she has. She's worked so hard to get to where she is now and Bill has been so supportive. They are such a nice couple; we're so blessed to call them friends," Walt's Mom said.

"I agree. I had a great time tonight. I'm glad we don't have too far of a drive home though. I haven't seen it rain like this in a very long time."

"Watch out! There's someone standing in the road!" she screamed.

He had just enough time to react. He jerked the steering wheel hard to the right. The car careened sideways and the front tires were already in the gravel when he pulled the steering wheel hard, back to the left. The car fish-tailed left, spraying gravel into the ditch and beyond. The car was back on the road but now headed for the other ditch. He pressed on the brakes and turned the steering wheel to the right, coming to a stop in the middle of the road. He pulled slowly on to the shoulder to regain his composure. He looked in his rear- view mirror but there was no sign of the man that had been standing in the road.

"You okay?" he asked.

His voice was shaky and his eyes were still wide.

"I'm fine. What the Hell was that? Who would be out in this weather? You'd think that they would have the common sense to stay off the road at least," she said.

"Yeah. I don't know, but I don't see him now."

"We should go back and check, just to make sure he's okay. I don't want him getting hit or getting somebody killed, trying to avoid him."

"I guess you're right," he said, and turned the car around.

They went slowly back in the direction that they had come, until they were positive that they had gone past where they had seen him. He turned the car around, and headed for home.

"I don't know. When we get home, I'll call the police and tell them to come and check it out," he said.

"That was some fancy driving back there," she said, reaching over to hold his hand.

"Thanks. Let's just get home, shall we?" he said.

"I'm with you."

He headed for home. His heart rate was starting to get back to normal. He would never tell her this, but he was sure that they were going to die back there. His thoughts drifted and he didn't see the tall slender man in the Armani suit, standing in the middle of the road, until the last second. He swerved to his left, but when he went to correct to the right, the wheels slid on the slick pavement and he headed straight for a tree. He glanced quickly at his wife, but he didn't even have time, to tell her that he loved her. The car came to an abrupt stop when it hit the base of the tree. The sound of breaking glass and water hissing from the radiator mixed with the sound of the howling wind and the pouring rain. A loud clap of thunder rolled across the sky.

The steering wheel was crushed into his chest. He turned his head to see his wife but she was no longer there. She had been thrown out of the car on impact. He struggled to remain conscious but his injuries were too great, and blackness overtook him.

Walt sat up straight in bed.

"What's wrong?" Elise asked, from beside him.

"I thought I heard something."

He looked at his alarm clock, and the display read 12:45 A.M.

The doorbell rang again, only this time there was no doubt what it was. Walt turned to look at Elise. Neither of them needed to speak. They knew what the sound of the doorbell meant. Walt jumped from the bed and Elise was right behind him as they went out into the hall.

They could see the blue and red lights from a police cruiser reflecting off the walls. Walt's heart sank. There was no question in his mind as to why they were here. His pace slowed and he walked carefully down the hall. He could hear his Grandma talking to one of the officers. He couldn't hear what they were saying but he knew at that moment what they had to tell her.

"No, No. Oh my God no! Are you sure?" she asked.

Walt could hear that she was crying. When he came to the end of the hall, he saw his Grandma slumped on the floor, with her head resting on the wall. She turned her head to face them and she held her arms out, as they rushed to her and she hugged them tightly. They spent the next few minutes that way. No words were spoken and none of them noticed when the policemen finally left.

Walt couldn't believe this was happening. He could believe it was happening, he knew all day that this moment was coming, or at least he was worried that it was coming. It was the fact that he had to live through this moment again; that's what he couldn't believe.

All doubt was removed now, about whether his dream was real or not. Elise was beside herself, wondering how he could have had a dream foretelling this event. Walt didn't tell her about Joshua. He didn't think that he wanted to share that part of the story with her, but because he didn't tell her that part; she thought that there were some other-worldly forces at work. Walt thought that she wasn't wrong about that, but he kept it to himself. Elise was with him every step of the way and this time he leaned on her for support, instead of pushing her away.

It was certainly no easier going through it a second time. In fact, in some ways it was much worse. Just the fact that he had to go through it for a second time, was bad in itself. The first time through was a dress rehearsal of sorts. He hoped that he had learned enough, that he could avoid making the same mistakes again, but only time would tell. The only positive thing in the whole scenario, was that he and Elise were tighter than ever, and that in itself, was worth the price of admission.

It was such a surreal experience. He had already grieved for his parents and here he was doing it again. He had been back for less than twenty-four hours and they were gone. It was sure nice to see them though. If he could do it over again, he would spend the entire day with them and he would make sure that somehow, they never went to the party at Sharon's. He had forgotten just how badly his Grandma had taken the news. She was an absolute basket case and it hurt him a lot to see her that way. The pain for him was different. He was already beginning to process his feelings about what had just happened.

He missed his parents, but he missed them before as well. Time had healed those old wounds and even though they had been re-opened, they began to heal much quicker this time. He wasn't the angry young boy that he had been the first time. This time, even though he looked like he was only twelve on the outside he was actually a couple months shy of his twenty first birthday. The fact that he had already lived through it once and the fact that he had many more years of experience to draw on then the first time, completely changed his outlook on the entire experience.

Walt helped his Grandma through this difficult time. He found it hard to believe that they made it through the first time, when it was her looking after him. He guessed that people do what they have to, in order to survive. She must have stepped up her game a little back then, but he couldn't remember all the details. All he could remember from that time, was the sadness and the anger that he felt.

His parents were gone again and he settled into his new life. In the beginning, he found that he was trying to remember what he did the first time; like there was some sort of script that he was supposed to follow. As time passed and he became more comfortable, he began to just live and forget about trying to remember what he did or how he acted the first time. After all, wasn't that what got him in trouble in the first place? It was certainly better to go a different route this time anyway.

Things were much different already. He and Elise were closer than ever and the huge chip that he had on his shoulder wasn't there this time.

He wondered whatever happened to Joshua. He said that he

would be here to guide him along the way, but so far, he hadn't seen neither hide nor hair of him. He didn't need him at this point anyway, so maybe that's why he hadn't been around. Maybe he only showed up when he was needed. In any case, his life was going just fine at the present time and he was so glad that he made the decision to start over. Except for the bumpy start with the loss of his parents, everything else was nearly perfect.

He was beginning to have a hard time remembering his old life though. He could remember the highlights. He remembered Joshua, sure enough. He remembered his parents dying, going to jail and being separated from Elise, but all the small stuff in between, was beginning to fade. He began to think that even that wouldn't be so bad. He had a chance at a new, happy life and he could do without all the bad memories from his previous life.

That fall and winter Elise spent a lot of time at his place. He wanted to stay close to home because he was worried about his Grandma and he didn't want to leave her alone. Her parents understood. They were devastated as well by the loss of his parents and they offered Walt and his Grandma as much support as they could.

By the springtime, Walt had only vague recollections of his previous life. That was both a blessing and a problem. On one hand, it was good that he had forgotten most of the bad things that had happened to him. On the other hand, he could have benefited from the experience that he had gained the first time through.

Walt's Grandma started to act like her old self and she started to enjoy life again. That's not to say, that they didn't all have their moments when they missed his parents, but they moved on with their lives as best they could.

The next year was just a normal year in the life of a thirteen-year-old boy. Nothing out of the ordinary happened. He got good marks in school, he read lots of books, he played sports and video games and he hung out with Elise and his other friends as much as he could. The year flew by and before he knew it, he was getting ready to start his first year of high school.

CHAPTER FIVE

He was big for his age and strong as well. He decided to try out for the football team. The school wasn't very big and so they only had one team for all ages. The chance of him making the team in his freshman year was slim but he was determined to try his best anyway. As it turned out, he just happened to be a very good football player and he made the team easily.

He still hung out with Elise every chance he got, but lately she had been spending more time with Abe, the captain of the football team. There was something that he didn't like about him. He couldn't quite put his finger on it but it was just a feeling that he got about him. He figured that if he made the football team then he could keep an eye on him.

"I don't know what it is. It's just a gut feeling I guess, but there's something about Abe that just doesn't sit well with me," Walt said to Elise, one day when they were walking home from school.

"Don't worry. I'm a big girl and I can take care of myself. He's just a friend anyway. I wouldn't even call him a friend actually. He's just always around when we have cheerleading practice. He probably thinks that it's his right as the captain of the football team, to sleep with all the cheerleaders. Believe me, I have only one guy on my radar," she said, and winked at him.

The next couple of years continued much the same way. Walt played football and Elise continued to be part of the cheerleading squad. They both did very well in school and they still spent time together almost every day. Walt never had a girlfriend the entire time and Elise never had a boyfriend and that was okay with Walt. He didn't know how he would cope with her having a boyfriend and he was glad that it hadn't come up yet.

It was a day much as it had been a couple of years before. They were talking about Abe again and Walt mentioned how he never really liked the guy. There was just something about him that rubbed him the wrong way.

"This seems like a conversation we've had before. Are you jealous?" Elise asked.

"I don't know what it is. There's just something about him that gives me the creeps," he said.

"Me too, but I told you before, I only have eyes for one guy. I remember the first time we talked about this. I told you then, that there was only one guy on my radar."

"Yeah, I remember," Walt said.

"It seems that you are either not interested or you are really bad at taking hints. I've dropped so many hints over the years that I'm about done with that. I'm just going to come right out with it. I'm eighteen and I'm done high school this year and so are you. I'm still a virgin, because I've been waiting for you and I think I'm going to go crazy if I have to wait any longer. What does a girl have to do to get laid around here?" she said, louder than she should have.

Walt took a quick look around to see if anyone had heard Elise's outburst. There was no one within earshot. Walt didn't know what to think. Sure, they had messed around a bit, but he thought that they were just playing. They had been friends his entire life, but he always had it in the back of his mind, that someday she would just leave him behind. He guessed that maybe it was because she was a year older than he was and he thought that he was just a little kid in her eyes. As they got older that year difference mattered less and less, it seemed. He was still a little taken aback by this new revelation and he wasn't sure what to say. He didn't say anything.

"You're not going to say anything?" she asked.

His cheeks turned red, but still said nothing.

"Cat got your tongue?" she teased, and put her arm around his neck.

"It's just that, when we were growing up, I thought that you might think of me as a little kid," he managed.

"Well we're nearly grown up and I'm still here. You might be younger but you are more mature than most guys my age, besides you're in the same grade as me anyway. Of course, if you're not interested; if I'm just wasting my time.... Let me know and I'll try to find someone my own age," she said, teasing him.

"Of course, I'm interested. Are you kidding me?" Walt said, excitedly.

"My parents are going to one of my Dad's friends for dinner. You can come over and study if you want," she said, making quotation marks with her fingers.

"I'll be there. Should I bring anything with me?" he asked, nervously.

"Bring a school book if you want. I'll tell them that I'm helping you with a book report. You don't need to bring anything else. I have us covered," she said.

He said goodbye to her and continued to his house. He didn't know what to think. He was scared. He was nervous. He was happy. He was excited.

He had a couple of hours to kill until it was time to go to Elise's place and it seemed like forever.

He went into his room and picked out a book for his so-called book report and then placed it on top of one of his school books. He went out into the living room to see what his Grandma was doing. It wasn't that he was overly interested in what she was up to; he just needed to pre-occupy his thoughts with something other than Elise.

"Hey G-ma. What are you up to?

He had always called her G-ma. He recalled asking her why he called her that, when he was younger. She wanted him to call her that because she said she was too young to be a Grandma. She wanted something that was different, something that reflected her unique personality. She figured that it was also a way of differentiating her from his other Grandma.

"Just watching my soap opera hon. It's getting good. Why? Do you want to watch it with me?" she asked, laughing.

She knew that he had no interest in watching one of her soap operas. They did however, watch T.V. together some evenings, if Elise wasn't over, or if he wasn't in his room reading or playing video games.

"No, I'm good thanks. I have to go over to Elise's tonight. She's going to help me with a book report."

He blushed a little as he said it and he could feel that he was beginning to get hard. He turned away from her, so that she wouldn't see, but she was too involved with watching her show and she never looked up, so thankfully she never noticed.

"Oh, that's nice. She's a wonderful girl, smart too. I bet that she'd be able to teach you a thing or two, if you let her," she said.

"That's what I'm hoping for," Walt said, laughing.

"Well, have a nice time. Are you going to be here for supper then?"

"Yeah, I'm going to head over after supper."

"Okay then. I don't mean to be rude, but shhh. This is getting too good to miss."

"I'll see you at supper, then," he said, and went back to his room.

Well, that killed all of ten minutes. He still had nearly two hours to waste and he needed something to do, to keep his mind off tonight.

He settled on playing a video game and between the action and talking to his friends online, it seemed to do the trick. Before he knew it, his Grandma stuck her head into his room and announced that supper was ready.

He had two hours that he had wasted and now he was short for time. He had to eat and then get ready. He wanted to have a shower and wear something decent, but he settled on eating supper and then just heading over as he was. He didn't want to arouse suspicion. He figured that it was all in his head, but he felt like everyone knew what he planned to do tonight. He tried to act normal during supper but he failed miserably, as far as he was concerned. His Grandma didn't seem to care; she was too busy going on about her soap opera to notice that he was acting strangely.

He ate quickly and then went back to his room. He changed his mind. He decided that he had better put on something a little nicer, after he showered and brushed his teeth. He ran through the shower and then picked out some decent clothes. He started down the hallway, then spun around and went to the bathroom to brush his teeth; almost forgot.

When he was done and he deemed himself presentable, he made his way down the hallway again.

"Okay, I'll see you later G-ma. Leave the dishes and I'll get them when I come home."

"I don't mind. I have an hour to kill before my show comes on. Go on, get out of here and don't forget your books. You have homework to do. It's important that you get a good education."

"Shit! I forgot. Thanks G-ma."

"Language!" she said.

"Sorry G-ma."

"Don't be too late. I worry when you're out too late, after dark."

"I won't be."

She didn't have to tell him why she felt that way. He knew why she worried. Ever since his parents had died, she was worried sick when he was out after the sun went down. He did his best to not push it too long after dark. On occasions that he needed to be longer, he tried to have Elise or his friends come to his place instead, so that she wouldn't have to worry.

He went back to his room, grabbed his books and left.

He had made the bike ride to Elise's house countless times before, but this time was completely different. He was so nervous that he could hardly pedal his bike. His hands were slipping on the grips of his handle bar. He had to keep wiping the sweat from his hands, onto his jeans. He tried to convince himself, that it was just Elise and that there was no reason to be nervous. Elise knew everything about him. She knew him better than his Grandma, better than his own parents had. She knew what scared him and what made him laugh. She knew that he was nervous around other girls, but that he felt completely confident and comfortable around her. She would know exactly how he was feeling, as soon as she saw him. He hoped that she wouldn't think that he was too big of a dork and call the whole thing off. He was after all a year younger than her and she could get anyone that she wanted. She was probably the most beautiful girl in the entire town. She was athletic and she had long, perfect legs, with blonde hair and blue eyes. She had perfect teeth, a cute little nose and a warm smile. She was bubbly, but not to the point of being annoying. She was, as far as he was concerned, perfect. It wasn't just him that thought this way. All his friends thought that she was hot and all the guys on the football team did as well. He still couldn't believe that she was interested in him. Sure, they had been friends their entire lives, but until earlier in the day, he just assumed that she would grow tired of him some day.

The ride to Elise's house usually took five minutes. Today it took him nearly ten. He was caught between taking longer to get there and trying to compose himself, and just hurrying the hell up, so he wouldn't get more nervous.

When he did get to her house, her parents were still home. He really hoped that they would have left before he got there. He felt like just riding past her house and waiting down the road, until they left. He turned into her driveway however, and leaned his bike against the front steps, like he always did.

Elise's parents were in the kitchen when he went in. He didn't knock, he just walked in. When he was younger it felt foreign to him to just walk into someone else's house without knocking. They insisted that he was just as much a part of the family as they were and that he didn't need to knock. This was the first time in years, that he had even thought of it. Usually, it never crossed his mind. Tonight however, was different. He felt as though everyone knew. He felt guilty and he felt as though it showed all over his face.

"Hey Walt, how's it going?" Bill asked.

"Good, I guess," Walt said, trying to downplay how over the top excited he was to be here.

He could tell that it was written all over his face. As soon as you leave, I'm going to get your daughter naked and we are going to have sex. I can't wait. I'm so excited that I can barely stand here and have a conversation with you. My legs feel rubbery and I feel like I might hyper-ventilate and I'm sweating beyond belief. I wish that you and Sharon would hurry the fuck up and leave before I faint. That's how I am tonight, thanks for asking. How are you?

"Oh, hey Walt, didn't hear you come in," Sharon said.

"We had better get going, we don't want to be late," Bill said to Sharon.

"I know. I'm nearly ready. Just have to grab my purse and a sweater and then we can go."

"Elise is just getting out of the shower. She'll be down in a bit. Just make yourself at home. You know where everything is," Bill said.

"Okay thanks."

Sharon and Bill left and Walt sat down at the kitchen table, waiting for Elise to finish her shower.

"You can come up," Elise called, from the bathroom.

"Okay. You want me to just wait in your room for you then?" Walt asked.

"You can come in," she said.

Walt slowly opened the bathroom door and went in. Elise was still in the shower, so he closed the lid on the toilet and sat down.

"I had to have a shower. I was so nervous that I was sweating all over. You can come in if you want," she said.

"I am in. I'm sitting right here."

"No, I mean you can come in," she said, opening the shower door, sticking her head through and smiling at him.

She closed the door and started to talk again.

"It's weird you know. We've known each other our whole lives and it isn't like we haven't messed around a little before, but I have to confess, I'm nervous as hell," she said.

Walt was in the process of taking off his clothes. He had just showered but he was already sweaty again. He too was nervous as hell, but he also knew, that there was a naked girl on the other side of that door. A naked girl that was very hot and that had just invited him in. He was willing to try and overcome his nervousness.

"I am too, but I'm still coming in," he said, and she laughed.

Walt opened the door and got in the shower. Elise was just finishing washing her hair, she was facing him but she had her eyes closed. The suds and water were running down the length of her body, making her skin glisten. Walt could hardly believe that he was standing naked in front of her. He unconsciously dropped his hands to cover his privates. He was shocked by her beauty. He had messed around with her on several occasions, but mostly when they were younger and they had always had their clothes on. Now he was standing looking at her naked body. Her perky breasts stood out perfectly, her tan lines accentuating them beautifully. He followed her tanned mid-section down to her tiny waist...

"Like what you see?" Elise said.

Walt looked up, to see that she was looking at him, and smiling.

"Very much," he managed.

"You should kiss me," she urged him.

Walt leaned forward and kissed her on the lips.

"No. I mean kiss me," she said, stepping forward, out of the full stream of the water.

She wrapped her arms around his neck and covered his mouth with hers. Her tongue flicked at his, and he followed suit. She pressed her body against his, and his rock-hard penis settled against her upper thigh. He wrapped his arms around her waist and pulled her closer to him, but no matter how tight he held her, she continued to be too far away from him.

Elise reached up and grabbed one of his hands and then the other. She guided them to the small of her back. They lingered there for a second before sliding down and coming to rest on her butt. He squeezed it gently and continued to kiss her. He could tell now that she was smiling and he stopped for a second to look at her.

"Finally. I've been waiting for this day forever," she said, and then resumed kissing him.

She reached down with her right hand and grabbed hold of his penis. He flinched slightly at first and then a smile ran across his face. She chuckled slightly and then continued to stroke his penis up and down. He began to thrust slightly, forward and back, moving his penis through her closed hand. He couldn't stop moving if he had wanted to, it was as involuntary as breathing, and at this point, stopping wasn't even an option. She tightened her grip and with her other hand she guided his hand toward her vagina. He pushed his index finger forward and felt the warmness inside her. She pulled back.

"Easy. Just rub here," she said, positioning the tip of his finger on her clitoris.

"Right there. That's it," she said, as he lightly rubbed his finger back and forth. "Little circles. Yeah, like that," she said, and Walt did as she asked.

She began to moan a little and he began to rub quicker as he got more excited.

"Just keep doing what you were doing, don't change it," she said.

Walt tried to do as she asked, but he was getting close to coming and he was having a hard time concentrating. Finally, he could hold off no longer. Elise rubbed her pelvis against him as he came on the inside of her thigh. He moaned a little and pushed back as she continued to stroke his penis. The tip of it was now so sensitive that he had to pull away from her. She laughed.

"I win!" she said.

"Now if you don't mind, kind sir," she said, guiding his finger back to her clitoris.

Walt gently rubbed it like she had showed him. He circled around and around, until she began to moan with pleasure again. She pressed her mouth hard against his and probed his mouth looking for his tongue. His penis was already hard again and he couldn't help but rub against the inside of her thigh. She grabbed him more tightly and she began to thrust her pelvis against him, moaning more loudly now. She reached her hands around and grabbed his butt and squeezed tightly. Her body became rigid and she was now moaning loudly and gasping for breath. Walt continued to rub her clitoris and she pushed her butt out and crossed her legs to stop him. She was coming and she stopped him, so that she could enjoy the moment. She held him tightly and she whispered in his ear. Her body was tense and she was shaking uncontrollably.

"I love you, Walt."

"I love you too, Elise."

She held on to him for a couple of moments, until her legs no longer felt rubbery.

They rinsed off quickly, dried off and then hurried into her bedroom.

"Get your clothes, in case my parents come home."

Walt ran back into the bathroom, scooped up his clothes and returned in a flash. Elise was lying on her back with her hands beneath her head and her knees up. Walt climbed up onto the bed and lie down beside her. Elise rolled toward him, wrapped her arms around him and then rolled back on to her back, so that he was now on top of her. Elise kissed him and Walt eagerly kissed her back, then he stopped.

"I'm not too heavy on top of you?"

"Just kiss me you fool," she said, laughing.

Walt did as she asked, as he cupped one of her breasts in his right hand. That uncontrollable urge to thrust his pelvis had returned and he began to rub his penis on her pelvic bone. Elise turned her head so that Walt's face was by her ear.

"Kiss my ear, and neck, my whole body," she said, panting a little.

Walt did as she asked; first kissing the outside of her ear and then flicking around it with his tongue. He moved to her neck and kissed it, running his tongue down, until he came to her shoulder, where he paused for a moment to kiss, before moving to her breast. He licked around her nipple with his tongue, first one way and then the other. Elise was breathing heavier by this point and a few moans of pleasure escaped her. He sucked gently on her nipple before moving down to kiss her stomach. He kissed his way down until he got to just above her vagina and then he kissed his way up her inner thigh until he reached her calf.

"Come here," Elise said, pulling him back on top of her.

Walt lie on top of her and began kissing her. His pelvis started to move again and after a couple of gentle thrusts, the tip of his penis slid into her wet and welcoming vagina.

"Wait! We need protection," Elise said.

She squirmed so that she could open the drawer on her nightstand. She opened the drawer and rummaged around with her right hand until she found what she was looking for. She produced a little plastic packet containing a condom, and handed it to Walt.

He grabbed it from her and then sat on the bed so that he could see what he was doing. He fumbled with it trying to get it open, but his hands were sweaty and he couldn't grip it tightly enough.

"Give it here. I've waited long enough," Elise said, laughing a little.

Elise grabbed the packet and ripped it open with her teeth. She took out the condom, oriented it the right way and then rolled it on to Walt's penis and then lie back down on the bed.

"Come, come," she said, motioning with her hands for Walt to get on top of her.

"Take it really slow. I've used a lot of toys. I mean a lot," she said, and laughed. "But I don't know how the real thing is going to feel. I'll let you know."

Walt got up on his hands, positioning the tip of his penis at the opening of her vagina and then pushed forward slowly. He watched her for any signs of discomfort. Her head was turned slightly to the side and she was smiling but her brow was all scrunched up.

"Are you sure it's okay?" Walt asked.

"It's more than okay. You can go in more," she said, panting a little.

Walt pushed in a little farther and he was amazed by the soft warm feeling of the inside of her vagina. He couldn't believe that this was happening. A smile spread across his face. If he died right now, he would die the happiest man on earth. Walt moved slowly out and then back in. Elise stopped him with her hands.

"Not so far in," she said.

Walt continued to move in and out, in long controlled strokes. Elise was moving her pelvis up and down to match what he was doing. He felt embarrassed that he was going to come so quickly, but he couldn't help himself. It was the best, most intense feeling that he had ever experienced. The combination of him moving in and out, her moving her pelvis up and down, along with her beauty and the little moaning noises that she was making, was just too much for him to handle. He tried to think of other things, so that he could last longer, but it was futile. He came and then continued moving in and out, hoping that she wouldn't notice. After a few seconds of uncertainty, he was able to continue on as before. This time he could enjoy it more, without the fear of coming too quickly.

He lie down on top of her and began kissing her again. He reached around with his right hand, grabbed her butt, squeezed it and pulled her into him. This time she allowed him to push his penis all the way in, and she moaned a little as he did. Elise slipped her right hand in between them. Walt lifted slightly to give her some room. She rubbed her fingers back and forth and around in circles, gently massaging her clitoris. She began to moan a little. Walt continued to thrust in long, even strokes and she began to moan louder and louder. She reached around with her free hand and grabbed his butt and pulled it toward her as she thrust her pelvis harder against him. She was now panting and moaning louder than ever, until she came. She now had both hands on his butt and pulled him tightly against her as she thrust her pelvis against his. She held him that way for a moment, with her body rigid and not moving, before relaxing and falling to the bed. She wrapped her arms around his neck, kissed him and he eagerly kissed her back. For the moment, he had forgotten about moving his pelvis in and out. He was content to kiss her and enjoy the moment. His eyes were closed but he could see her, just as well as if they were open. He could see her beauty and it still astounded him, that she had picked him. He loved her. He didn't know if he had ever thought of it before. She was a friend to him and of course he loved her, but this was different. He loved her so completely, as a man loves a woman. He was so lost in thought, so caught up in the moment that he never noticed the slender black man in an Armani suit, standing in the corner of the room. How long he had been there, no one knows, but one second he was there and the next he was gone.

Chapter Six

"That was amazing. I was so nervous. I don't know if you could tell. I've been waiting for this moment for years. I've had a lot of practice with toys, but nothing prepared me for that. I feel so comfortable with you. I guess because we've been friends for so long and we know each other so well. I thought that the first time would be weird and awkward but I think it went very well, don't you?" she asked.

The smile on his face told her everything she needed to know. Walt wasn't sure that he could stop smiling if he wanted to. She was right though. It was so much better than he could have imagined. He was so nervous at the start that he was sure he was going to mess everything up.

"I agree. That was absolutely amazing. How did you know what to do? I'm sorry, I sound like such a dork. It's just that it felt so natural, not at all what I was expecting."

"I've been waiting for this day for years. A girl's got to do what a girl's got to do. Sometimes I got so horny, I thought I would explode. So, I experimented a lot. Oh God, that sounded a little creepy. You know what I mean."

"I know what you mean," he said, squeezing her a little tighter.

"See! I told you that we could never drift apart. You're stuck with me forever and that's just the way I like it. I can't ever imagine not having you in my life," she said, squeezing him back.

Walt lie there enjoying the moment. He couldn't seem to stop smiling. He didn't want to leave, but he thought that he had better be gone before Elise's parents got home and before G-ma began to worry. There was no way that Elise's parents wouldn't know that something was up. He would never be able to hide what was going on in his head.

"I can't wait to tell my parents," Elise said.

"What! Are you crazy?"

"Not about this, Eww. No, I was talking about us, silly," she said.

"Oh," he said, chuckling.

"Actually, I want to surprise them. The next time you come over, I'm just going to plant a huge kiss on you, right in front of them."

"Sounds fun. It will definitely surprise them."

"I can't wait for the whole world to know that we're together; you know?" she said, beaming.

Walt couldn't wait either. He would be proud to call Elise his girlfriend. All the guys would be so jealous.

"I know exactly how you feel," he said, and squeezed her tightly.

He never wanted to let go of her. He felt closer to her than ever before, but still he felt as though she wasn't close enough. He was so incredibly happy, that he felt as though he would explode and he knew that she felt the same way.

And they lived happily ever after, the end…… not quite.

Walt and Elise lie there for a long time, enjoying the closeness, neither of them wanting to move. As time passed, their internal clocks told them that they had better get going, before her parents got home.

"I hate to say it, but I think we had better get moving. We have a book report to do," Elise said, laughing.

Walt laughed. "Yeah, I think we should," he said reluctantly.

"Oh shit! G-ma's going to be worried sick."

"She'll be fine. She knows that you are at my house."

"Ever since my parents died, she freaks out if I'm out too long after dark," Walt just finished saying, and then the phone rang.

"Hello. How are you? Yep. He's just about to leave. The book report took longer than expected. He'll be right home. Bye," Elise said, and hung up the phone.

"Told you."

"Okay. I guess you had better get going, but we are definitely doing this again, as soon as possible," she said, kissing him, then getting out of bed to get dressed.

"How about now?" Walt said, getting out of bed and standing in the middle of the room, showing her his hard on.

Elise laughed. "I'll have to take a rain check. Now cover that thing up before you get us both in trouble."

Walt got dressed and walked with her to the front door.

"I hope this doesn't change anything between us," Elise said.

"This changes everything. No, that didn't come out right. I know what you mean. We are still first and foremost best friends, but now I feel closer to you than I could have ever imagined," he said, grabbing her and kissing her passionately.

She hugged him tightly. "You'd better go. I love you," she said in his ear.

"I love you too. I'll see you in the morning," he said, got on his bike, and rode home as quickly as he could.

His Grandma was sitting watching the television when he got home. She was trying to act casual, but she failed miserably. Walt walked over to her and gave her a big hug.

"Sorry G-ma. I lost track of time. My report took longer than I expected."

"No need to apologize. You're a good boy. It's not you, it's me. You know how I am. Ever since your parents passed, I've been so paranoid when you're out after dark. I know it's crazy, but I just can't seem to get past it," she said.

Walt just squeezed her shoulder.

"I know G-ma."

He was thirsty, so he went to the refrigerator, grabbed the orange juice, drank a couple of large swallows from the carton and then went into the living room and sat down on the couch with his Grandma.

"So, you got your book report done then?"

"Yep. It went better than expected," he said.

"That's good."

They sat in silence for a while, watching some show that he couldn't care a less about, but that she found to be entertaining.

"Well, I'm going to my room. I'll see you in the morning."

"Okay, good night dear."

He went into his room with the intentions of playing a video game but he had only one thing on his mind tonight, and that was Elise. He texted her, just to tell her that he was thinking about her and then flopped on his bed. She texted him back a bunch of hearts, followed by xoxo and then: until next time.

He couldn't wait; but until then he was just going to chill. He decided against playing a game and instead turned on his T.V. He underestimated how much of a toll the night had taken on him and he was fast asleep before he knew it.

In his dream, he was in a back alley and there was someone else there, but he had his back to him and he couldn't make out who it was. It was as if he was watching a movie, and the camera was above them. He could tell that he was talking to the other person but couldn't hear what they were saying. This version of himself was older, he had tattoos on his arms and his hair was longer. He was smoking a cigarette and he had a scruffy beard. There were dark circles around his eyes and he looked very unhappy. The other man produced a handgun and held it out to him, which he took hesitantly.

"Good night dear. I'm going to bed. Make sure you turn off your T.V. please, before you go to sleep," his Grandma said, through the closed door.

Walt just caught the last of what she said, as he began to wake up.

"Okay G-ma. Good night."

Walt thought about his strange dream. It was funny how the mind worked, he thought. Dreams of Elise should have been first and foremost in his mind. He dismissed his dream and thought of Elise, as he drifted off to sleep.

When he woke up the next morning, his first thoughts were of Elise. He could see her standing naked in the shower and then lying on her bed. Gorgeous! The next thought was of the strange dream he had. It seemed familiar somehow, as though he had experienced it before. It was a fleeting thought however and he quickly dismissed it. Elise was all that he cared to think about right now.

He said good morning to his Grandma and then got ready for

school.

"I'm leaving now. I'm going over to Elise's for breakfast."

"Okay hon. I'll see you after school."

"See ya."

Walt jumped on his bike and hurried over to Elise's. He threw his bike against the front step and went inside. Sharon and Bill were at the table having a coffee and toast.

"Good morning, how's it going today, Walt?" Bill asked.

"Good thanks.

"Hi Walt," Sharon said.

"Good morning Sharon."

Walt could hear Elise coming down the stairs. He turned toward her.

"You forgot your books last night," she said.

She set the books on the edge of the table and walked over to him. She threw her hands around his neck and pulled him into her body and gave him a nice long kiss. At first Walt was surprised, but then he remembered. Elise stepped back from him and looked in the direction of her parents. Walt followed her gaze. Sharon's cup of coffee was suspended a couple of inches from her mouth and Bill was sitting with his mouth slightly ajar. Sharon set her cup down on the table.

"Something you two want to share?" Sharon asked.

"Well, it's like this Mom. I'm not getting any younger and I've never had a boyfriend, so I thought that Walt could do double duty. He can be my best friend and my boyfriend. I figure if he's good enough to be the one then he's good enough to be the other. I guess I should have talked to you about this. Are you alright with this Walt?" she said.

Walt didn't say anything. He was just looking at her parents and waiting for some sort of reaction.

"You mean to tell me, that you decided this on your own, without talking to Walt. Elise, you should know better," Sharon said.

Elise started laughing and Walt followed suit.

"Really funny. So, you aren't together then?" Sharon asked.

"Oh, we're together alright. I was just having some fun, that's all."

"Oh Elise! You're incorrigible! So, when did this happen," Sharon asked.

"I've been thinking about it for quite some time and I finally told Walt how I feel, the other day."

"And, how do you feel about this Walt?" Bill asked.

"I love your daughter and I would do anything for her. I know we are the happiest when we are together, so I figure why not be together all the time. Besides, we already know each other so well. We can always be ourselves around each other."

"Well. I can't argue with that kind of logic. I'm happy for you two. I couldn't ask for a better fellow to be with our Elise and if she's happy then we're happy," Bill said.

"Oh. Come here you two," Sharon said, putting her arms around the two of them and hugging them.

"Come on, Mom. You're so embarrassing!" Elise said.

"I'm just so happy for the two of you. You make such a cute couple," Sharon said.

"Okay Mom, sorry I said anything. We're going to grab something and go sit out back."

"Okay. The two love birds want to be left alone. We understand. Go ahead," Sharon said.

Elise just rolled her eyes. She grabbed some fruit and some toast and dragged Walt down the hall and out onto the back patio.

"Sorry about that. I wouldn't have said anything, if I knew she was going to be like that."

"It's fine. She was fine. It wasn't that bad really," Walt said.

They sat holding hands while they ate their breakfast. When they were done, they went back into the house. Walt drank a glass of orange juice and Elise had a glass of milk. He grabbed his books and they left for school. Neither Bill or Sharon said anything, except for good bye. Sharon probably didn't want to push her luck and Bill was generally a quiet man as it was.

When they got to school, Elise kissed him and they went their separate ways. He took a quick look around to see if anyone was watching. He hoped that they were. He couldn't be prouder, to call

Elise his girlfriend. He didn't see anyone but that was okay, he thought. Everyone would know soon enough.

There was one person that did see. Actually, no; better make that two. Abe Warren, the asshole captain of the football team, saw Walt kissing Elise. He thought that he should be with the prettiest girl in school. He figured it was his right as the captain of the football team and he didn't like it one little bit.

The other person to see was a little farther down the street. Nobody saw him, or at least no one noticed him. He didn't stand out or draw attention to himself. There was nothing remarkable about him or unremarkable for that matter. He was just a sharply dressed, slender black man, walking down the street and he went completely unnoticed.

CHAPTER SEVEN

"That was a Hell of a game you played the other night," the stranger said, walking out from behind the bleachers.

"Thanks mister. Yeah, we played a great game," Abe said.

"Oh sure, the team. No; I mean you. You played one Hell of a game. No need for political correctness around me," Joshua said.

"I don't want to brag, but yeah, I think I played one of my best games this year. Are you a reporter or something?" Abe asked.

"Oh, I'm something alright. No, just a fan is all."

"Well, nice talking to you. I had better get going."

"That your girlfriend over there? She sure is a pretty little thing. I guess it comes with being captain of the football team. Just one of the added perks," Joshua said.

"Elise? No, she's always with Walt. I'm not sure what their deal is, but they are always together."

"It's been my experience that in small towns, the captain of the football team is king and can do pretty much whatever he wants. I'd say that the prettiest girl in town should be with the captain of the football team. Don't you agree?"

"I guess, but she made her choice. I've asked her out a few times and she said no."

"Oh son, you have a lot to learn. If you want something in life, you have to take it. Anyway, I have to get going, so I'll see you around," Joshua said, then turned and walked away.

Abe stood thinking about what the stranger had said. He was right. Elise should be with him. He had always liked her. What wasn't there to like? She was smart and friendly and hot as Hell. Abe stood and watched as she walked with Walt. Her long, lean, muscular legs swinging freely from beneath her yellow miniskirt. They stopped with her back facing him. The wind blew her skirt up a little, revealing the full length of her leg, and it was stunning. The stranger was right. Abe had to have her.

Elise put her arms around Walt's neck and gave him a long kiss. It wasn't a kiss that one friend would give another. There was no mistaking it for what it was. What the fuck! What does she see in that guy anyway? he thought. He spun around in disgust and walked away.

"So, how was your day?" Elise asked, when they found each other after school.

"I couldn't concentrate. I spent the whole day thinking about last night," Walt said.

"I know, right? I did the same thing. Listen, I promised the girls that I'd go to the party tonight with them, but I'll see you once I get there. Maybe we can sneak off and be alone for a bit. If you know what I mean?" she said, smiling devilishly.

"I wouldn't miss it for anything. I have to go to practice but I'll see you later," Walt said and kissed her, before running off.

"Okay, me too. Later. Can't wait!" she called after him.

Walt's head wasn't really into practicing and apparently, it didn't go unnoticed.

"Hey! You want to get your head in the game. We have a big game coming up on Tuesday and I want everyone on the same page," Abe barked at him.

Walt didn't respond. He just moved away from him and continued as if he hadn't said anything. Abe seemed a little off. He was always an asshole, but this was different. A couple of times during practice he caught him glaring at him from across the field. He wasn't sure what his deal was, but he kept his distance, in an attempt to avoid a confrontation. He just wanted to get through practice, get to the party that night and see Elise.

Elise looked for Walt briefly after practice, but didn't see him, so she went home and started to get ready for the party.

Walt went home, had a shower and then went out with a buddy and had a burger and fries. His buddy's brother got them some beer and they were all set for the party.

The party was in a bush lot at the edge of town. Everyone either had to drive or ride their bikes. Walt elected to ride his bike, to avoid hassles getting home. He told his Grandma that he was staying at a friend's, so that she wouldn't worry. He only needed to make the obligatory call to wish her a good night later and he was free to enjoy the rest of the night. He definitely felt like celebrating tonight. He was pumped to spend more time with Elise. He couldn't believe how excited that he was to be with her. The difference in the way he felt about her now, versus a couple of days ago, was like night and day.

Elise didn't feel much like eating. She had some cheese and crackers and a pickle. She was far too excited to eat. It was the strangest thing. She had known Walt her entire life, but for the last two days, she couldn't think of anything but being with him. She, Hailey and Ashley all got ready at her house. The bulk of the conversation was of course about her and Walt, and how excited they were for her. She definitely felt like celebrating tonight. Hailey had already gotten the drinks and Ashley's Mom was going to pick them up afterwards, so they were all set. This was going to be a great night. She could just feel it.

Abe had been stewing about it all day. He never really liked Walt and it bothered him that a girl as hot as Elise, was wasting her time with him. He honestly couldn't understand why it bothered him so much. It was like a seed was planted when he talked to that guy earlier and it continued to grow and grow. He was right about one thing. He did deserve to be with the hottest girl in town, not Walt. He still had some running around to do, and picking up some liquor was tops on his list. He drove down to the convenience store beside Yu's Chinese restaurant and parked his car on an angle so that no one would park too close. He drove a 1968 Mustang. His Dad gave it to him as a present, when they made him captain of the football team. It was red when his Dad owned it, but Abe had it painted black recently and he didn't want any scratches on it.

Abe got out of the car and there was already a group of dads gathering to admire the car.

"Oh, hey Abe. I didn't realize that it was you. Nice car man! Hey, great game the other night. I'll be there watching the game on Tuesday. Hopefully you stick it to those guys as well," Rory said.

Rory was a local that never left their small town. He used to play high school football and he still went to every game. He could talk football for hours and hours.

"That's the plan. I don't mean to be rude but I'm kinda in a hurry," Abe said.

"Yeah, no, I understand. Good luck on Tuesday," Rory said.

The other two guys were still admiring the car. "Go Cougars!" they yelled, as they walked to their cars.

Abe responded by giving them a fist pump. "Fuck Yeah!" he yelled.

Abe finally made it to the door of the convenience store. He caught Mr. Yu out of the corner of his eye. He was always trying to get Abe to explain the rules of football to him. He came to every game and handed out menus in the crowd and gave away free fortune cookies. Normally, Abe would humour him for a while, but tonight he didn't want to be bothered. He just wanted to get in, get out, and go on his merry way.

He pretended he didn't see Mr. Yu. He flung open the door and quickly entered the store. The door hit the bell above the door hard and it went rolling across the floor. Abe closed the door and scooped up the bell, in one graceful movement.

"Sorry about that. I guess that I must have opened the door too quickly," he said, as he stood up.

"Hey that's no problem. I'm sick of hearing that bell anyway," the cashier said, holding out his hand, to take it from him.

"Hey, you're the guy from earlier," Abe said.

"Joshua's the name. Pleased to meet you," he said.

Abe dropped the bell into his left hand and shook Joshua's right hand. A blue spark jumped from Joshua's hand to his. He jumped a bit, but then shook his hand anyway. His hand felt like warm butter, but he had a firm handshake all the same.

"Static, I guess," Abe said, laughing nervously.

"It happens," Joshua said.

Joshua's voice sounded like music. He had noticed it a little, earlier, but now he really noticed it. It was such a soothing voice. He could probably sell snow to an Inuit, Abe thought.

"You work here? Haven't seen you here before."

"Yeah, just started the other day. I guess the guy that was working here didn't show up for work for three days; so, the job just kinda fell into my lap. Lucky for me," Joshua said.

"A little over-dressed, aren't you?" Abe asked.

Joshua was wearing a dark green suit with pin-stripes and an apron over top of it.

"I suppose so. It's just that I'm used to dressing this way. Old habits die hard, I guess. I don't really need the money. I just like to see the people that come in here. I like to meet new people, and this gives me a chance to do just that."

Abe walked down the aisle, looking for whiskey. He grabbed a bottle and turned to go back to the counter. When he turned, he nearly bumped into Joshua, who had followed him.

"Jesus! You scared the shit out of me!" Abe yelled.

"Sorry 'bout that. I just thought you might need a hand. I have a knack for knowing what people need, even when they're not entirely sure themselves."

"I'm good. I've got what I came for," Abe said.

"I seem to recall a certain lady, that would probably appreciate it, if you bought her a drink or two," Joshua said.

"If you're talking about Elise; she's going with Walt," Abe said.

"Oh, I see. Hmm."

"What?"

"Oh, nothing. When I met you, I figured you for a don't take no for an answer, kind of guy. I figured that you had more fight in you;

that's all. Guess I was wrong."

"I am. It's just…What do you propose?" Abe asked.

"The way to a girl's heart is through her friends. If they like you, then you're better than half-way home. I'd buy some coolers for the girls and have a few drinks with them. You know, get on their good side," Joshua said.

"Can't hurt, I guess. If it doesn't work, then at least I can have one of them."

"That's the spirit! Girls love a confident man. You deserve to have any girl you want. Just remember that," Joshua said.

Abe grabbed a bunch of coolers and his whiskey and took it to the counter.

"How much do I owe you?" Abe asked.

"I'll tell you what. The next time I see you. You tell me that you got the girl and we'll call it even. If you didn't, then you can pay me then. How's that sound?"

"Sounds fair to me. You know, you're alright. You're a good guy," Abe said.

"We're the same, you and me. There's one thing I know and that's people. I'm in the people business, you might say. Hey, listen, have a good time tonight."

"I will. Thanks mister. "

"Call me Joshua."

Abe was no sooner out the door and Joshua turned the sign on the front, from open to closed and locked up. He had a couple of errands to run and he didn't want to be late.

• • •

Jared had to work late. He hated closing during the week. It was Wednesday and no one ever came in, during the middle of the week. There were always a few people of course but not enough to help pass the time. Friday and Saturday nights were different. He didn't mind working then, as long as he didn't have to close. It was the best job in town if you wanted to know where all the parties were. He couldn't wait until Friday night. There was going to be a huge party at a bush lot, just out of town. All the cheerleaders were going to be there and he was hoping that one of them might get drunk enough to find him attractive. He knew that it would take a lot of booze, but hey; a guy can dream, right?

He finished cleaning up, locked the front door and walked through to the back. He grabbed a beer out of the cooler for the ride home and then locked the back door. He opened his car door and started to swing his leg into the front seat, when he caught some movement out of the corner of his eye. He jumped a bit. A shot of adrenaline coursed through his arteries.

"Oh, hey. Didn't mean to startle you. I'm new in town. I don't see very well, especially in the dark. I must have gotten turned around somehow and now I find myself in a dark alley. Could you point me in the right direction? I live on Maple," the stranger in the suit asked.

He seemed harmless enough to Jared. He had a calm, friendly demeanor about him and he certainly was no bum, based on the way he was dressed.

"Maple's clear across town. I think it's the last street, right before the gravel pit. If I'm not mistaken?" Jared said.

"Yes, that's right. So, which way?" Joshua asked, pointing in both directions.

"I'll give you a lift, if you want. It's out of my way but I'm in no hurry. No one's waiting for me at home."

"Not married?" Joshua asked, as he got in the car.

"God no! I just moved here myself not too long ago. I bought a place over on Pine street with the inheritance that my Mom left me. No, it's just me, all alone."

"Well. I appreciate what you're doing for me," Joshua said.

"Hey no problem. I'm happy to help. Like I said, I have no place to be."

"It must get lonely being all by yourself. I know how it feels. I could use the company if you want to come in and have a few drinks?"

"Sure. Why not?" Jared said.

They rode in silence until they got to Joshua's house. Joshua let them in and immediately went to get a couple of glasses with some ice.

"Pick your poison. I have whiskey, vodka, gin and beer." Joshua said.

"Give me a beer I guess."

They started with one drink and then another and before Jared knew it, he had consumed more beer in one sitting, than ever before. He liked Joshua. He was easy to talk to and he felt like he could tell him anything. He was telling him things that he had never told another living soul. He knew down deep, that Joshua was a man that he could trust.

"Listen. I make a life out of reading people and if you don't mind me saying; you seem like a man that's down on his luck. I know that there's something that you want to get off your chest. It's weighing on you so heavily that you feel at times that it will suffocate you. I also know that you are wondering why you should be talking to a complete stranger about this. Who better than a stranger? You can tell me anything and I won't judge you. You have my word on that, and whatever you tell me, will stay between us. You have my word on that as well," Joshua said.

Jared sat looking down at the table for a minute. He took a long swig of beer and then sat motionless again, before looking up at Joshua. Tears were streaming down his face.

"I know. It's hard. It's not your fault. Sometimes things don't go according to plan. Sometimes life doesn't go the way we want it to," Joshua said, reaching out and clasping him on the shoulder.

A blue spark leapt from Joshua to Jared.

"I couldn't help it," Jared said.

"I know. It's not your fault. Listen, to make you feel better I could tell you my hard luck story or you could tell me yours. When we are done exchanging stories, I can offer you a solution. How does that sound?"

"If it's true, it sounds good to me," Jared said, wiping the tears from his eyes.

"Of course, it's true. I wouldn't lie to you. Now, do you want to start, or shall I?" Joshua asked.

"I will. I want to get it off my chest."

Jared recounted his story about having to move across the country, trying to out-run the memories of what he had done. No matter how far away he got, the memories just wouldn't let him be. It started nearly a year ago, and it went on, until six months ago. He just couldn't resist any longer. He knew it was wrong, but he couldn't help himself. Every day he watched these two beautiful young girls walk by. He lived a block away from the school and they walked by at the same time every day. He tried to find things to do each day when he knew they would be walking by. He tried not to think about them, but the more he tried not to, the more he did. He watched porn so much that it started to interfere with his job and he was on the brink of being fired from work. It was all in an attempt, to try and subdue his real urges. He did everything in his power to control himself, but eventually he couldn't.

"I didn't want to hurt those two little girls. They were so special, so pretty."

"It's not your fault," Joshua said, reassuringly.

"Those two girls are dead because of me. I can't live with what I've done. I didn't want to kill them but I had to. I couldn't have them telling on me. They said that they wouldn't but they would have. I know they would have. I wish I could bring them back, but I can't. It's not just them. Imagine the pain that their families are going through. Why? Because I couldn't control my urges," Jared said, breaking into tears again.

Jared continued to talk through his tears, but the words were unintelligible. He was sobbing and running his fingers through his hair, pulling it out in clumps. He began banging his forehead on the table, in a futile attempt to make the memories go away. When he had calmed himself a little, and the tears had slowed to a trickle; Joshua began to speak again.

"I'll tell you my story and then you can decide what to do," Joshua said.

Joshua told Jared the same hard-luck story that he had told Walt, years before. Joshua showed him the scars on his temples as proof, but Jared barely looked at them. He was eager to get the .38 pistol out of his hand. He couldn't wait. For him it was more about going back and seeing those two girls alive again. It was more about stopping the hurting, than it was for him to get a second chance. Jared reached for the gun but Joshua pulled it back from him.

"Not here. Let's go down into the quarry. That way no one will hear us," Joshua said.

Jared agreed eagerly. He couldn't wait to do it. He was anxious to get a second chance.

Once they had reached the bottom of the quarry floor, Joshua produced the hand gun. Jared reached for it impatiently but Joshua pulled it back from him again. He went over the ground rules and then handed him the gun. A blue spark jumped from Joshua's fingertips to his. He barely noticed, he was too focused on the gun.

"I can go back and do it over again. I mean I can change things, so those two girls don't have to die?" Jared asked.

"Absolutely. Free will. You'll get a second chance," Joshua said.

Jared didn't fool around. He didn't ask any more questions. He put the .38 to his temple, smiled and pulled the trigger. His limp body slumped to the gravel floor of the quarry. He twitched a couple of times, blood pumping from the small hole in his left temple and gushing from the larger hole in his right. Joshua stood over top of him, waiting for him to stop twitching and for the blood to stop flowing. When he was sure that both had stopped; he reached down, picked up the gun and put his hand on Jared's body. A blue spark jumped from Joshua's finger tips to Jared's forehead. Instantly the large pool of blood and Jared's body were gone. Joshua looked across the dark floor of the quarry and then up at the stars shining brightly in the heavens. He took a long, deep breath and let it out slowly. Another night, another job well done. He smiled, turned and went back home.

CHAPTER EIGHT

When the three girls were ready, Ashley's Mom drove them out to the party.

"You girls have your cell phones, right? Be careful, try not to drink too much and stay together."

"Yes Mom. Hey, let us out here. I don't want people to see you drop us off. It's embarrassing," Ashley said.

"Too bad. I'm dropping you off right out front. You shouldn't be walking around in the dark, out in the country. You never know what can happen. Call me when you want me to pick you up, otherwise I'll be here at 1."

"Okay," Ashley said.

"Thanks, Mrs. Bennett," Elise and Hailey said.

They walked off the road and past rows and rows of cars, parked in a large clearing.

Abe was just getting out of his car when they walked past.

"Good evening ladies."

Ashley and Hailey smiled and said hi. Elise just waved.

"You guys want a drink? Might as well get this party started," Abe said.

"Sure, why not," Hailey said.

Elise shot her a look. She just wanted to get into the party, so that she could find Walt. She grabbed Hailey's elbow and held her back.

"Let's just go. You can talk to him later, inside," she whispered in her ear.

"One drink, come on. This is my party too," Hailey said.

"Okay, one drink," Elise agreed.

They went over to Abe's car. He had the trunk open and there was a cooler full of bottles on ice. He handed each of the girls a drink and poured a whiskey for himself. He slugged it back and poured another one.

"You girls need a ride home after. I'd be happy to give you a lift," Abe said.

He said you girls, but he was only looking at Elise when he said it.

"Not if you're going to be drinking like that; besides, Ashley's Mom is picking us up," Hailey said.

"Well, I brought a tent to set up, in case I've had too much to drink and I have to stay the night."

Elise looked at Ashley and Hailey. They were both smiling at Abe and they didn't seem to notice, that every time that he spoke, he was only looking at Elise.

Elise drank her cooler quickly and then urged her friends to leave.

"Come on Elise. One more drink isn't going to kill you. Walt probably isn't even here yet; we're early," Hailey said.

Elise looked at Ashley for support, but it seemed that she was content to stay where she was and drink at the back of Abe's car, for now.

"One more drink and then we'll get going," Ashley said.

Abe grabbed another cooler from his trunk and handed it to Elise. She didn't like the way he held onto the bottle, just a little too long and stared at her while he did. She just grabbed the bottle and then went to stand beside Hailey.

•   •   •

Walt slowly made his way out of town toward the party. He had to stop a couple of times to adjust his beer that kept trying to fall. He pulled on to the gravel alongside the roadway for the third time, trying to find a better way to secure the beer to his bike. He was focused on what he was doing, and didn't notice the gentleman walk up from behind him.

"Having some trouble there?" Joshua asked.

Walt jumped and he dropped his beer in the gravel, but luckily none of them opened.

"You scared the shit out of me!" Walt said, and looked around.

He was wondering why a guy dressed in a suit would be wandering down a country road after dark, or at any time for that matter.

"Oh, sorry 'bout that. I have a way of sneaking up on people, I guess. Looks like you're having a bit of trouble there. I'd offer you a ride but my car broke down just up the road a way," Joshua said.

"No problem. Yeah, I never heard you coming," Walt said, and stood looking at him.

It was dark, so he couldn't get a good look at him but he seemed very familiar to him. It wasn't just the way he looked. It was his voice as well.

"Have we met before?" Walt offered.

"No, I don't think so. I usually remember a face. I'm kind of in the people business, so I would probably remember."

"It's just that you seem really familiar, that's all," Walt said.

"Maybe in a previous life or something," Joshua said and chuckled.

"Yeah, maybe," Walt said distractedly, still trying to secure his beer to his bike.

"My name's Joshua," he said, holding out his hand.

Walt was a little frustrated. He could use a bit of a break anyway, so he set the beer on the gravel and turned to face Joshua.

"Nice to meet you Joshua. My name's Walt," he said, shaking his hand.

A tiny blue spark jumped from Joshua's fingertips and into Walt's.

"Did you see that? That was cool," Walt said.

Joshua's hand felt warm and soft. Walt felt a little self-conscious, by how long he held Joshua's hand. He hoped that he didn't notice. It was kind of weird, but he couldn't help himself. It was a soothing feeling. That was the only way to describe it. It was like pulling a warm and cozy blanket out of the dryer and holding it next to your skin.

"Here let me help you with your bike. I know a thing or two about tying knots; maybe I can help," Joshua said.

"Sure, that would be great! I can't seem to get it to stay. It keeps falling off."

Joshua reached down and grabbed hold of Walt's bike. Another blue spark jumped from his finger tips and into his bike.

"You sure have some static electricity going on there," Walt remarked.

"I guess so. There you go. That should hold it," Joshua said when he was finished tying the beer onto his bike.

"Thanks. That looks better than the way I had it."

"Don't mention it. Have fun," Joshua said, as he turned to walk down the road.

"Did you call for help for your car? Do you need me to make a call?" Walt asked.

"No. I have it covered. Thanks though."

Walt hopped on his bike and headed in the direction of the party. He passed by what must have been Joshua's car, pulled off on to the shoulder of the road. He had that strange feeling again, that he had met him before. He dismissed it and kept riding up the road and around the bend. He could see lights from the party, a few miles up the road.

Walt felt as though it was becoming harder and harder to pedal his bike. He looked down and noticed that his tires were nearly flat. He pulled off onto the gravel to check them and by the time he did, the front one was completely flat and the back one had come off the rim. Great! Now what was he going to do? He was already late. He struggled with trying to untie the beer but the knots were too tight. At this point he couldn't give a shit about the beer anyway. He just wanted to see Elise. He grabbed a couple of beers, threw his bike into the ditch and started to walk in the direction of the lights and the party.

• • •

Down the road behind him, Joshua climbed into his car, turned on the ignition and put his car in drive. When he rounded the first bend he turned on his lights and headed for home. Another night and another job well done, he thought.

• • •

Walt walked at a brisk pace, but even at this speed, it was going to take him forty-five minutes. The lights of the party looked deceivingly close. He thought that he was nearly there when he started walking and that was twenty minutes ago. It was a lot farther than he had originally thought. He began to think about Joshua. He just couldn't shake the feeling, that they had met before. Maybe he just had a way about him that made him feel familiar. Whatever it was, he felt comfortable around him. He seemed like a very nice gentleman.

Elise, Hailey and Ashley had moved into the party, but at Elise's insistence, they stayed in a spot close to the entrance from the road. Elise looked around when they first got there, but couldn't find Walt. Now she wanted to be by the entrance, for when he finally did show up. Abe was still hanging around, and Ashley and Hailey were happy to let him give them drinks. Elise had a couple as well, but the other two were several drinks ahead of her. Abe poured some whiskey into a glass and handed it to Elise.

"Here, have a swig, it'll help you relax. Walt will be here soon, if he isn't already. You might as well have a little fun while you're waiting. I'll go with you. We can take another look around to see if he's here and if not, we'll come back here," Abe said.

Elise was hesitant, but thought, what the Hell and downed the drink. Turns out that there was more whiskey in the glass than she had thought. She put her hand over her mouth and had to fight from puking it back up. That was it, last drink until Walt gets here, she thought.

She started walking with Abe in the direction of the bonfire and

Hailey and Ashley followed.

"You guys had better stay here in case Walt shows up, and don't split up. Stick together. You've had quite a bit to drink and I don't want to see anyone take advantage of you," Abe said.

"Okay. We won't let anyone take advantage of us until you get back, Abe," Hailey said, giggling.

Elise turned briefly toward Hailey and Ashley to make sure they were staying and then walked with Abe again. She had never really had a problem with Abe, it was Walt that had a strange feeling about him. Right now, Abe was being a perfect gentleman. They walked slowly through the party, looking for Walt and asking if anyone had seen him. So far, nothing.

Elise could really feel the alcohol starting to hit her. She probably should have eaten something before she came but she really hadn't intended on drinking so much. She reached out to grab Abe's elbow for balance and he put his arm around her to steady her.

"Come on. Let's sit you down before you fall over," Abe said.

Elise sat on a log by the fire. She watched as the flames danced and swirled sending hot embers drifting up into the night sky. She followed them up, up with her eyes. She felt dizzy from tilting her head back so far. She brought her head forward again and the dizzy feeling stopped but the heat from the fire was making her feel sick.

"Are you feeling okay? You look like you're going to be sick," Abe asked.

"I'm hot. I need to get away from this fire," she said, trying to stand.

Abe helped her to her feet and they walked away from the fire.

"How's that? Is that better?"

"I just want Walt to get here. I need to sit," she said.

"There's no place to sit here. Come with me," he said, and took her farther away from the fire, to where there were a few tents set up.

"Here, you sit here and I'll go look for Walt."

Elise sat down in the tent with her feet hanging out the door while Abe went to find Walt.

He's being so nice and helpful, she thought. She decided to lie back and just rest for a while, until Walt got there. She pulled her feet and legs inside the tent and lie down. The bottom of the tent was nice and cool on the back of her bare arms. She lay there, hoping that Walt would be there soon and that he wouldn't be upset with her because she had gotten so drunk.

Abe left the tent but it wasn't Walt that he went to find. He found a couple of his buddies drinking by the fire.

"Hey guys, if you see Walt don't tell him where Elise is. She's with me and I don't want to be disturbed. If you know what I mean?" Abe said.

"Sure thing, you lucky son of a bitch," Trent said.

Abe went back to the tent and found Elise lying inside.

"Is that you Walt?" she asked, slurring her words.

Abe didn't say anything. He just knelt in the entrance of the tent and stared at her.

"I'm glad you're here. I hope you're not mad at me for getting so drunk. You should help me get out of these clothes. I'm still too hot, and the bottom of the tent feels really nice on my bare skin," she said, struggling to take off her shoes.

Abe looked up at her, she looked as though her eyes were still closed. He removed the one shoe that was still on and then removed her socks.

"That's nice," she said, with her eyes still closed. She sounded like she was on the cusp of falling asleep or passing out.

She used all the strength she could muster, to lift her legs into the air, so that he could remove her pants. He let her legs fall gently onto the floor of the tent. She moaned a little, clearly enjoying the coolness against her bare skin.

"Come, come," she said, motioning him forward and then letting her arms drop at her sides, too heavy to hold up any longer.

Abe hesitated. There was the girl of his dreams, half-naked in front of him. She was so stunning, so beautiful. He had dreamt about this moment for a long time, but not like this. Then he recalled the conversation that he had with Joshua. The seed that he planted, had taken on a life of its own. He was right. He deserved to be with the prettiest girl in town. Besides, he didn't like that prick Walt, anyway. He pulled her panties down around her ankles, loosened his belt and hiked his pants down around his knees.

Walt finally got to the party. He saw Hailey immediately and went to talk to her.

"Hey Hailey. Where's Elise?" Walt asked.

"Heyyyy Walt!" She yelled, turning and then stumbling toward him.

She threw her arms around him and hugged him. He could smell the strong smell of alcohol on her breath. She was clearly drunk.

Walt pried her off him, and held her at arm's length.

"Where's Elise?

"She's with you," she said, and started laughing hysterically.

"Obviously not! Where did you see her last?" Walt asked, impatiently.

"Oh yeah. She went with Abe, to find you," she said, and pointed in the direction of the fire.

He took off toward the fire, without saying another word to Hailey. She stood for a minute, looking in the direction that he had been, a few moments before. When she realized that he was gone, she turned and walked slowly toward a group of people to her left.

Walt found Ashley by the fire, with a couple of other girls, but not Elise. He saw Trent and Chuck on the other side of the fire, so he went over to them.

"Hey. Have you guys seen Abe?"

"No, man. Not since we first got here," Chuck said.

"How about you Trent?"

"No, not for a while," Trent said, looking over Walt's shoulder to a group of tents behind him.

Walt turned and looked in the direction that Trent's eyes had drifted.

"You want a drink Walt?" Trent asked.

"No. I'm looking for Elise."

"She's around. Come on, have a drink with us. She'll turn up,"

Trent said.

Walt ignored him and walked quickly in the direction of the tents. The first two he came to; the zippers on the doors were open, and there was no one inside. The third tent's zipper was closed and he could hear movement inside.

"Elise?" Walt called.

"Walt?" Elise called groggily. Followed by: "What the fuck?"

Walt ripped open the zipper of the tent and found Abe on top of Elise. Elise was struggling to sit upright, but she was having difficulty doing so. She was clearly drunk, more so than Hailey. She fell on her back and was unable to get up. Abe scurried to pull his pants up. He managed to get them as far as his knees, before Walt jumped him and started raining punches down on him. He hit him in the side of the face and knocked him over on his back; then he was on top of him punching him in the face, over and over again.

Trent and Chuck showed up and pulled Walt off Abe. They took one look inside the tent and understood immediately what had happened. They let go of Walt and grabbed hold of Abe and dragged him out onto the ground and threw him on his back. Chuck kicked him as hard as he could in the side of the ribs, while Trent stood over him, shaking his head. He removed his phone from his pocket and called the police.

Walt closed the door to the tent and put Elise's clothes back on her. She was trying to talk, but she was slurring her words so badly, that he couldn't make out what she was saying.

Walt wanted to kill Abe, but his first priority was Elise and keeping her safe. He helped her out of the tent, scooped her into his arms and began heading for the road. Chuck and Trent had a hold of Abe and they were dragging him in the same direction.

Walt was nearly at the road and he could hear the wail of sirens coming. Before too long, the dark of the night was awash with the white lights of an ambulance and the blue and red lights of a police cruiser, not far behind.

Several girls that had heard what had happened came up and slapped Abe in the face. He struggled to get free but Chuck and Trent had him held tightly.

"Sorry man. Never thought he was capable of something like this," Chuck said to Walt.

"You have nothing to be sorry for. My only concern is for Elise right now. Keep that asshole away from her!" Walt yelled.

They dragged Abe far away from where Walt was standing; still holding Elise.

The ambulance pulled up and he gave her to the paramedics. They examined her quickly, asked Walt several questions and then they all went to the hospital. As they drove away, he saw a policeman putting cuffs on Abe and putting him in the back of the cruiser.

His attention quickly shifted back to Elise. She was still passed out and Walt figured that was a good thing. He wasn't sure how much she was awake for and he shuddered at the thought. He knew Elise. Even though she may have been unconscious for most, or all of it, that wouldn't matter to her. She was in for a tough time in the immediate future, and he hoped that he could do enough to get her through it.

Walt had to stay in the waiting room while they examined her, of course.

Hailey and Ashley showed up at the hospital shortly after they got there, but they were in no shape to be of any good to anyone, and Ashley's Mom took them home.

Walt stayed in the waiting room for an hour before they let him in to see her. In the meantime, a policeman showed up and took a statement from him. He waited until they were done their examination and then he took a statement from her as well. During this time, Elise's parents showed up and found Walt sitting in the waiting room.

Sharon came rushing over to him, grabbed him and hugged him tightly and cried and cried. Bill just shook his hand and sat down, with his eyes cast to the floor.

When the time came, the three of them went in to see Elise, together.

CHAPTER NINE

In the days and weeks to follow, Walt was with Elise as much as possible, of course that was nothing new. He had always felt so comfortable with her, but now he felt awkward a lot of the time. He didn't know what to say or how to act. Elise slept a lot. She didn't talk much. She was quiet and withdrawn and she rarely smiled. It hurt Walt to see her like this, but he had no way of helping her. Sharon and Bill took her to see a therapist and he was helping her work through things. Ashley and Hailey were there a lot of the time as well, trying to buoy her spirits, but even they had little to no effect on her mood.

Elise and Walt could talk about everything and anything. They were never at a loss for words, until now.

Elise appreciated all the support. She told everyone that she did, but ultimately this was something that she had to work through in her own way.

Months had passed and she seemed to be getting back on the right track. She was more talkative and began to smile once in a while. Walt and her, would sit for hours and have long conversations about anything and everything.

Then Abe's trial started, and you could see the toll it took on her. She thought that once he was behind bars, that she would finally feel vindicated, and would finally have some peace.

Walt, Elise, Trent, Chuck, Hailey, Ashley, Adam and Marissa were all called to testify at the trial. The trial lasted for two weeks and at the end of it, Abe was found not guilty. The jurors found that there wasn't sufficient evidence to prove, that the sex wasn't consensual.

Elise broke into tears when they read the verdict. Actually, there were more faces with tears on them then there were dry ones. Bill had to be restrained and removed from the courtroom, so that he wouldn't tear Abe apart. Walt felt a sick feeling in the pit of his stomach.

Elise sat slumped in her chair, covering her face.

As long as he lived, he would never forget the smug look on Abe's face. He had the nerve to smile and give the thumbs up sign to the people sitting and watching the proceedings.

Walt felt like climbing over the railing and strangling Abe himself, but his priority, was still and always, Elise. He went to her and held her and was soon joined by Sharon.

Elise stopped crying quickly, and then she wanted to go home. She had a hardened look about her. Walt wasn't sure what hurt him more, the sight of her crying, or the new look on her face.

She insisted that she was fine, and that she would just have to learn to put this behind her. Walt wasn't buying it.

Nearly two weeks had passed and she was still acting as if everything was fine, except that she hadn't gone back to school. A stranger would know that everything wasn't fine with her. Those that knew Elise, were certainly not convinced.

Abe was back at school and pretending like everything was as it was before. No one would talk to him however, and it wasn't long before he quit the football team. He went to classes and then went straight home and no one ever saw him out and about. Walt told Elise that he was being treated like a pariah, but it didn't seem to buoy her spirits at all.

In the beginning, Elise's parents had taken some time off work to be with her. Bill went back to work and then eventually Sharon had to go back to work as well. Walt took some time away from school, and now he was too far behind to miss any more classes.

"I appreciate all your help you guys, but I'm fine, really. I think the best thing for all of us, is to go back to our normal lives," Elise said, to the three of them.

●　●　●

She was going stir-crazy and she needed to get out of the house. When Walt left, she went for a walk. The fresh air and exercise would do her a world of good. She had no particular destination in mind. She just wanted to go for a walk, and would be happy if she didn't run into anyone on her way. She decided to go down by the river and sit by the water. The sound of the water rushing over the rocks was always soothing, and God knew, she could use something to soothe her now. She sat thinking about the many times that she and Walt had spent here as kids. In the summer, it was their favourite place to cool off, and to go fishing in the spring and fall. In the winter, they spent a lot of time, along with the rest of their friends, skating on the reservoir above the dam.

The water changed and moved, babbling quietly to her. It told her secrets, that she alone was there to hear. Everyone was at school or at work and she had the place to herself. All her troubles were washed away with the flowing water. She felt better than she had since that night before the party. She quickly thought of something else, anything but what had happened at the party. The first thing that came to mind was Walt of course. He had been so great through all of this. She loved him more than ever, but he wouldn't know that. She had been cold and distant. She knew that he understood, but she also knew that he deserved better. They hadn't made love since that first time and she still wasn't ready for that yet. She was ready to let him in again though. He was hurting too, it wasn't just her. Her parents were hurting as well and she knew that they were all waiting for her to get on with her life. They were all very patient with her, but it was as if they wouldn't allow themselves to be happy again, until she was.

"Hi there. I hope I'm not intruding, but I like to sit here by the water while I eat my lunch. I find the sound of the water very therapeutic. It's very relaxing. I'm sorry, I'm interrupting. I'll sit over there," he said, pointing downstream.

"No, it's fine, really," Elise said.

He seemed like a nice gentleman and she didn't want to be rude.

"No school today?" Joshua asked.

"No. I haven't been feeling well lately."

"I'm sorry to hear that. Well, you've come to the right place. I've always found that being by the water helps calm me. They say, that as the mind goes, the body will follow. Something like that."

"Yeah, even when I have a lot on my mind; the water seems to carry my troubles away with it," Elise said.

"Sounds like you have something on your mind. Sometimes it helps to talk to someone about it. I'm a good listener. I'm Joshua by the way," he said, holding out his hand.

"Nice to meet you, Joshua. I'm Elise. But, no, I don't want to talk about it," she said, shaking his hand.

She jumped a little, and let out a little scream. A blue spark of static electricity jumped from Joshua's fingertips to hers. She rubbed her fingers on her pants until the feeling returned to them.

"That was quite the spark," Elise said.

"Sure was."

They sat talking for a while. She was happy that he decided to eat his lunch with her. He had a way of making her feel comfortable, relaxed. He was very kind and funny too. She really liked him. She was having a really nice time, and she had completely forgotten about her troubles, but that all changed in an instant.

She stopped talking in mid-sentence, staring toward the other side of the river.

Joshua followed her gaze and saw that Abe was standing across the river. He was still quite a way away, but there was no mistaking who it was.

Abe lifted his arm and waved in her direction. Elise wanted to cry. She wanted to scream. She wanted to wade across the river and gouge his eyes out. How dare he wave at her like they were friends. She couldn't believe the nerve of him. What she didn't know, was that it wasn't her that he was waving to.

"Oh, that's that Abe fellow. He's the captain of the football team. Can't say as I care much for him. I was talking to him the other day at the store. I remarked about how sad it was, that that young girl had been raped a few months ago. That bastard should have been put away for a long time, instead he got off. Pardon my language, but it makes me angry. He was making light of it. He said that she had it coming to her and that she was just a tease. He went on to say that he would do it again, if the opportunity presented itself. That's when I realized, that he was, that guy. Well, I threw him out of my store and told him to never come back. I couldn't believe his arrogance, his smugness. I hope that he gets what's coming to him. Terrible, just terrible," Joshua said, shaking his head.

Elise couldn't take it, she jumped up and screamed at the top of her lungs. She didn't scream any words, just a long, blood curdling scream, directed at Abe across the stream. Abe turned and made a hasty retreat.

"That was me! That was me, he was talking about!" she said, through tears of rage.

"Oh, my dear. I'm so sorry, I didn't know," Joshua said, enveloping her in his arms and hugging her.

Elise allowed Joshua to comfort her. It felt right somehow and it seemed to calm her. Joshua put his cheek on the side of her head, to hide his enormous smile. Right on time Abe, he thought, right on time.

"There, there. Everything will be alright. You'll see," Joshua said, stroking her hair with his hand.

"I wish he would die. I can't believe how smug that son of a bitch is," she said, letting out another small scream.

"If the law isn't going to do something about him, then someone should. Where I'm from, they had ways of making people like him go away. Permanently, if you know what I mean," Joshua said.

He held her at arm's length, to look at her and wiped the tears from her eyes.

"These things have a way of working themselves out. You'll see," he said, kindly.

He took a pen out of his pocket, scribbled something on a scrap of paper, folded it and handed it to her.

"I have to get going or I'm going to be late for work. Are you going to be alright? I'll stay if you need me too," Joshua asked.

"I'll be fine."

"You should go straight home. I wouldn't be out alone with that animal still running around free," Joshua said.

"You're probably right."

"Okay, well if you need anything," he said, nodding toward the piece of paper in her hand, then turning and walking toward his car.

Elise sat for a minute, after Joshua had left. What a nice gentleman, she thought. Too bad there weren't more people in the world like him. People that just wanted to help. She got up and walked toward home. She didn't want to run into Abe, so she thought that she had better get moving. She kept looking over her shoulder, making sure that Abe wasn't following her. How long was she going to have to look over her shoulder? The answer was simple. As long as Abe was around, she would always be looking over her shoulder.

She unfolded the piece of paper. It read: Anything you need. I'll help. Followed by his phone number. The word anything was underlined and she was nearly certain, that she knew why. She was relatively certain, that he did mean absolutely anything.

CHAPTER TEN

Elise made it home without running into Abe and she was thankful for that, but the more that she thought about it, the more she knew, that she had to do something. She wasn't about to live her life, looking over her shoulder. Maybe Joshua knew some people that would put the fear of God into Abe, and make him move away or at the very least keep his distance from her. Days passed, and she could still see him standing on the other side of the river, smiling and waving, like nothing had happened. Walt was right to have had misgivings about Abe. She should have taken his feelings more seriously.

She was really starting to come around, before she had seen Abe at the river. All she could think about, was how smug he was. He had gotten away with it, and it was her that was suffering, while he continued to live his life. Oh sure, his life had changed as well. He wasn't treated like a God any longer, but he wasn't behind bars like he should be.

She decided to call Joshua. She wasn't sure what she would say, or what it was that she wanted him to do for her. She did know, that he made her feel comfortable and at the very least, he was someone that she could talk to.

"Hi... Joshua...it's Elise, we met a few days ago, at the dam," she said, hesitating.

"I know who it is. I've been expecting your call, Elise. I'm very pleased that you called. When would you like to meet? How about tomorrow at the dam? I have my lunch there at twelve o'clock, I'll see you then. Bye dear," he said and hung up the phone.

His voice was as calm, reassuring, deep and melodic as she remembered. He seemed to know what she was about to say, and answered before she had a chance to speak. It was better that way, anyhow. She wasn't sure that she would have been able to talk, without sounding like an idiot.

She got there a little late and he was already sitting, waiting for her when she arrived.

"It's good to see you again," Joshua said, getting up to give her a big hug.

"Come, sit right here," he said, brushing the dirt from the rock beside him.

"It's nice to see you too," she said and sat down.

"I'd ask you how it's been going, but I gather from the fact that you called me, that things could be better," he said, shrugging his shoulders.

"It's just that… when I saw Abe the other day, it freaked me out. The entire walk home, I was looking over my shoulder. I don't want to be looking over my shoulder the rest of my life."

"Understood. I can only imagine what you've been through. Good news though! We are going to change that, starting today. You swing by my place tonight and we'll come up with a plan. It will all work out in the end; I can promise you that."

"Thank you. I really appreciate what you're doing for me," Elise said.

"Happy to do it my dear. Someone has to stand up to the bullies of the world and it might as well be us," he said, patting her knee.

She took his hand in hers and thanked him again. She squeezed it lightly and then let it go.

"Tonight then. Where?" she asked.

"I live on Maple, 23, I think it is. This is kind of embarrassing, but I'm not entirely sure. I haven't lived there long. Just come by around seven. I'll be sitting on the front porch."

"Okay see you tonight," she said, hugging him, then taking off for home.

She wasn't as paranoid as the other day, but she still felt the need to check over her shoulder, every once in a while.

She felt guilty, and she hadn't even done anything yet. She lied to Walt, so there was that, she supposed. She had never lied to Walt before, at least that she could remember. Oaky, so there were little white lies that she told of course, but nothing of any consequence. This was the first time that she could ever remember, outright lying to him. She wasn't even sure why she did. Maybe she didn't want him to know that she was still scared. It made her feel weak and she desperately wanted to feel in control again. Walt would have understood and he would have been totally supportive. He also would have stopped her from making a mistake and doing something stupid. Maybe that's why she lied to him. Maybe she didn't want him to stop her. She told Walt that she had a migraine, that she was going to have a nap and that she would call him when she woke up. That would buy her a couple of hours. She wasn't sure how long she would be at Joshua's, but she figured that it would give her enough time. Enough time for what? She really wasn't sure, but she trusted that Joshua would make it better, somehow.

As she walked, she thought for a moment, that this probably wasn't such a good idea. Walt should have come with her. How much did she really know about Joshua anyway? What if something happened? Then she pushed those thoughts away. Joshua was a sweet heart. She could just tell that he was the sweetest gentleman and he would never hurt a fly.

She got to his place at five minutes to seven and he was sitting on the front porch as he said he would be.

"Close," he said, pointing to the 25 on the mailbox, and laughing.

He smiled and ushered her up onto the porch. After that, he was all business.

"We had better go inside. I don't want the neighbours hearing what we have to talk about," he said, quietly.

Elise reached into her pocket, to feel for the familiar shape of her cell phone, just in case she needed it.

Joshua walked into the dining room and pulled out a chair for her to sit in. Elise sat down and he sat across the table from her.

"So, we know why you're here, but we don't know why you're here. I know that you want to take back your life, but how far are you willing to go; that's the question. Listen to me, I'm sorry, I don't mean it to sound so ominous. I've been thinking. I believe that what you need, is to feel safe and not have to be looking over your shoulder all of the time," he said.

"That's exactly how I feel. I want to feel like I'm in control of the situation."

"Exactly!" he said, and then. "Exactly," a little quieter.

"I get excited sometimes. I want you to feel safe, and I believe that I have just the thing," he said, getting up and going to the hutch behind him.

It was made of dark wood, and it was intricately carved around the edges. There were two panes of glass in the doors on the front of it, that were frosted around the edges. It looked like the perfect blend of old and new. He opened the top drawer and retrieved a wooden box from inside. He set it on the table in front of him and then sat down again. He opened the box and spun it toward her. Inside was a .38 pistol. It was sitting in a mould that fit it perfectly. The interior of the box was lined with red velvet. The gun itself had a white handle that looked like quartz. It was a brilliant, glossy black, except for the trigger. The bluing on the trigger was completely worn away, leaving just the bare steel.

Joshua plucked it out of its cushioned holder, opened the action and spun it. Elise had never seen a gun up close before, but it looked and sounded like a revolver from the movies. Joshua held it out for her and she took it gently from his hand. A blue spark jumped from the gun to her hand. It scared her and she nearly dropped it. She laughed nervously and then gripped the gun a little tighter.

"Just relax. Feel the smoothness of it. Feel the weight of it. Open the action and spin it. Hear the noise it makes. How does it make you feel? It isn't something to be feared. It is something to be respected for sure, but guns don't kill people, only people kill people. Besides no one is killing anyone. It's for protection only."

"It makes me feel confident, brave. I like the weight of it. It isn't too heavy, but it feels like it has substance. It feels like it is part of me when I hold it."

"Go ahead, lift it and point it at something in the corner. Look down the barrel of the gun. Both hands. How does that feel?"

"Feels good."

"Now go ahead and pull the hammer back. Don't worry, it isn't loaded."

She did as he asked and she loved the feel of it. She was smiling from ear to ear. He showed her how to uncock it, and then how to load it as well. She was still smiling. She wouldn't have thought that holding a gun, would feel so empowering. There was no question that she had made the right decision to come here.

"So, what do you think?" Joshua asked.

"I love it," she gushed.

"I thought you might. Okay then. You want to come by tomorrow and I'll show you how to shoot it?" he asked.

"Absolutely! What time? I'll be here."

"Say, nine. How's that?"

"Sounds good to me," she said, excitedly.

"Nine it is then."

Elise hugged him, thanked him, then hugged him one last time, before she left. She was giddy with excitement. She couldn't wait until the morning, so she could shoot it. She could still remember how it felt in her hand. It felt like it was an extension of her arm and hand when she pointed it. It felt as if it had become part of her and she felt naked without it. She walked the entire way home, thinking about the gun and she never thought to check over her shoulder once. By the time that she got home, the giddy feeling had passed but she could still feel the gun in her hand. When she closed her eyes, she could still recall every magnificent piece of it. The way the handle looked and felt in her hand. The way the gun shone in brilliant black, except for where the trigger was worn to bare steel.

She slipped into the house and went to her bedroom, unnoticed. She lay down on her bed and stared at the ceiling for a while. She was waiting for the smile to fade from her face before she called Walt. She was supposed to be having a nap, because she had a migraine. It might draw some suspicion, if she was smiling like a Cheshire cat. When she was able to control the stupid grin on her face; she picked up her phone and called Walt.

"Hey. What are you up to? Just woke up a couple of minutes ago. Headache's gone," Elise said.

"That's good. Can I come over?" Walt asked.

"Sure. I'd like that."

"Be right over."

She held her phone for a while looking at it, before shutting it off and setting it on her nightstand. She really loved him. It was about time, that she showed him just how much. It seemed like seconds later, Walt was at her bedroom door.

"That didn't take long."

"I couldn't wait to see you. I miss not seeing you at school, eating lunch with you, walking to and from school with you. You know?" Walt said.

"Yeah, I do know. I was just lying here thinking the same thing. I want you to know that I really appreciate how supportive you've been. I love you and I think it's time that I start showing you."

"It's okay. There's no place in the world that I'd rather be, than right here. I love you too."

"Get over here!" she said, holding up her arms.

He walked into her outstretched arms and hugged her tightly.

"Lie down with me," she said.

Walt lie down beside her and she rolled over on top of him and started to kiss him. Walt kissed her back, hugging her tightly as he did.

"You have too many clothes on," she said, as she wiggled out of her top.

"I guess I do," he said, as he took off his shirt.

He lie back down on the bed and she undid the zipper on his pants and pulled them off.

"What about your parents?" Walt asked.

"They're watching T.V. They'll be busy for hours."

She lie down on top of him and started to kiss him again. She reached between them and grabbed hold of his penis and started to stroke it up and down. Walt rolled over on top of her and started to remove her pants.

Elise felt as though she couldn't breathe. She tried to find the words, to tell Walt to get off, but they wouldn't come. She could hear herself screaming the words in her mind, but she couldn't make a sound. She tried to roll him off, but her muscles were frozen and she couldn't move. Tears begun to roll down her cheeks.

Walt sensed that there was something wrong. He stopped kissing her and looked down at her face. She had a pained look on her face and she was crying. He jumped off her, knelt on the floor and held her hand.

"Are you okay?" he said gently, as he rubbed her shoulder with his other hand.

With Walt off her, she could breathe again. She took a couple gasps of breath and then began breathing normally. The enormous weight that she had felt was dissipating and she could start to move her legs again. She sat up and leaned toward Walt. She grabbed his face and kissed him.

"I'm so sorry. I don't know what happened. It was like I was paralyzed and I couldn't move. I was really scared," she said.

"It's okay. I understand. I think we need to take it a little slower, that's all. There's no hurry; I'm not going anywhere," he said and kissed her back.

"Maybe just a little playing around next time. It will be like old times when we were kids," she said, laughing nervously.

"Whatever you want. We'll go at your pace."

Walt put his pants back on and then lie down beside her on the bed. Elise lay her head on his arm and they cuddled and talked for a couple of hours.

"Don't you have to call your G-ma?" she asked.

"I told her where I was going. She seems to be okay, as long as she knows that I'm here."

"That's good. At least one of us has overcome their demons."

"Just give yourself some time. You have all the time you need, because I'm not going anywhere," Walt said again.

"Thank you... for everything. You're so good to me. I was thinking earlier that it might help if I went back to school, Monday maybe. What do you think?"

"I think that would be awesome! I can't wait to see you more. I've really missed you. I know I still see you every day, but I can never seem to get enough of you," Walt said, squeezing her tightly.

"I know, right? We've been together our whole lives. You'd think we'd be sick of each other by now," she said laughing.

It was so nice to see her smile and laugh again. It nearly broke his heart to see how sad she had been these last few months and as recently as a couple of hours ago. He wanted to take it slowly, to avoid a repeat performance of what had happened earlier. He could wait. She was worth waiting for.

Walt left and Elise lie on her bed and thought about what had happened earlier. It was proof that she still hadn't put this behind her and that she needed more time. She was still seeing her therapist once a week and that always helped her sort through things. Then she thought of earlier in the night and the feel of the gun in her hands. She loved the feel of it, but more than anything, she liked the way it made her feel. It made her feel confident, empowered and she wanted it with her now. My precious, she thought, and laughed nervously.

That night while she slept, she dreamt of Joshua and of course the gun. The shiny black of its barrel and the white of the handle, sparkled in the moonlight. Joshua held it out to her and she eagerly grabbed for it. He pulled it back from her, and she could feel the disappointment rising in her. She wanted it badly. It seemed to call to her. She wanted to hold it and she could feel that it wanted to be with her too. There were blue sparks shooting from it in all directions. She didn't pull away from them. She moved her hand closer and the sparks jumped to her fingertips and ran up her hand. They crackled and snapped, speaking to her as they did.

"We can be together. Come be with me. Embrace me. Love me. Until death do us part," they said.

Elise reached again for the gun and this time Joshua let her grab it. She pulled it tightly to her chest and stroked it lovingly. She was smiling from ear to ear, and she forgot that Joshua was even there. It was only her and the gun in the entire world, and nothing or no one else mattered.

In the morning when she awoke, the dream was still fresh in her mind. She remembered everything; from the way it felt, to the way it looked and the way it talked so lovingly to her. She couldn't wait to see it, to hold it again. She jumped out of bed and got ready quickly, far too quickly as it turned out. She had a lot of time to kill before going to meet Joshua and she had far too much energy to be idle. She jumped on her bike and rode over to Walt's. He wouldn't be leaving for school for half an hour or so.

She bounced by his Grandma, when she answered the door, and met Walt in the hall as he was leaving his bedroom. She pushed him back into his room and started to kiss him.

"What's gotten into you this morning?" he asked, when she finally let him breathe.

"I just woke up this morning in a great mood, with a ton of energy, so I thought that I would come share."

Walt smiled at her. He was pleased to see that her bubbly personality was back. He didn't know how long it would last, but he wanted to enjoy it while it did. Through all these difficult months, he only now realized that it had been missing.

"I'm just about to leave for school. You want to ride with me?"

"Sure," Elise said, looking at her watch, to make sure she had time.

They rode together and it was like old times again. Things were definitely looking up. She was going to take back control of her life, and that started with going to see Joshua and then going back to school on Monday. She couldn't be happier and she couldn't wait.

They talked all the way to school. Well actually, she talked and Walt listened. Walt didn't mind. He was just happy to see her in such a good mood.

They got to the school and Elise planted a long kiss on him and then she hurried in the direction of Joshua's house.

Joshua was sitting on his front porch, when she arrived.

"Top of the morning to you," he said, flashing an enormous smile.

"And good morning to you too, kind sir," Elise responded.

Joshua took a long deep breath; filling his lungs with the crisp, clean, morning air.

"It's a good morning to be alive," he said, and then produced a pipe from his pocket. He stuffed it, lit it and then took another long, deep breath and let it out slowly.

"Yup. It sure is a good morning to be alive," he repeated.

Elise didn't respond, but she agreed whole-heartedly. Joshua didn't seem to be in any hurry. He was enjoying the morning and his pipe, and he was content to sit right there until he was finished. She didn't want to be rude, but she had a hard time sitting still and not fidgeting.

"Are you alright my dear? It seems as though you have something on your mind?" he teased.

He knew exactly what it was. He could see the excitement in her eyes. He had seen it play out many times before. The gun had chosen her and she had chosen it. There was only one way that this could end now.

"So, what brings you by?" he asked. Teasing her again.

She had a moment of panic when she thought that maybe he had forgotten about today, or worse yet that, he had changed his mind. Then he flashed his infectious grin, and she was relieved to see that he was just playing with her.

"Come on in. I can finish my pipe as we walk."

She followed him into the house and into the dining room. The box containing the gun was already sitting on the table. He scooped it up and continued walking toward the back door. She felt a split-second of excitement, followed by bitter disappointment, when she realized that he wasn't removing the gun from the box. Elise followed him like a lost puppy, through the house, down the stairs and into the back yard. He slowed his pace and she quickly came up alongside him.

"I almost forgot. I didn't bring any ammo. I'll be right back," he said, handing her the box, turning and walking toward the house.

Joshua looked back over his shoulder to where she stood on the lawn, holding the box. He reached into his pocket to feel for the two boxes of shells that he knew were there. He smiled contentedly and then pressed on.

Elise never hesitated. She opened the case as soon as Joshua had turned his back. The sunlight glinted off the gun and she had to squint so that she could see it better. She turned her back to the sun and then opened her eyes again. There it was, nestled in its soft case, sleeping peacefully. She stroked it softly and whispered to it but it never responded. She closed the case slowly and then turned to see Joshua coming out of the house and down the steps.

"I must be getting forgetful in my old age. Plum forgot the ammo. Isn't much good without it," he said cheerfully, holding out his hand to take the case from her.

Elise handed him the case slowly, trying to hide her disappointment.

Joshua grabbed it and kept walking, without missing a beat. Perhaps she was a better actor than she had thought.

When Joshua left her with the box; he knew that she would open it. If there was ever any doubt, that doubt was completely removed now. The guilt was written all over her face. He knew that she wouldn't be able to resist it. Everything was as he knew it would be. She had fallen completely under its spell.

There was a small dirt trail that went from the back of Joshua's property to where the gravel at the edge of the quarry started. It had been abandoned for the better part of twenty years. There were no trespassing signs all around the perimeter, but no one paid them much attention. People rode dirt bikes in here and fished at the several ponds that had filled in with water over the years. On weekends, you could always find a group of teenagers partying down here or having sex in the backseat of their cars. The cops didn't bother anyone too much, as long as it didn't get out of control. Nestled into one of the high banks of gravel surrounding the old quarry, was a wooden frame that people used for target practice. This is where they were headed at the moment.

"Next time I come down, I'll have to remember to bring some tin cans with me. These ones are starting to look a little ratty," Joshua said.

Joshua set three of the cans atop the wooden frame and came back to stand with Elise. He was careful where he walked, to avoid the many shards of broken glass that lie everywhere. He held the case out for her to hold, while he removed the gun. He held the gun out for her to see. He opened the action, loaded it and then unloaded it. He took the case, handed her the gun, then dropped the bullets into her other hand.

He placed the case on the ground and watched as she loaded it. When she had finished, he took it from her. He showed her how to stand and how to hold it with two hands. He shot the three cans and hit all of them, right in the middle.

"Good shooting! You must practice a lot."

"Not really. It just came naturally to me."

"Oh. I just thought… because you hit them all … and I can see that the trigger is very worn; so, it's obviously been shot a lot."

"Nope," he said, simply.

He went to set the cans back on their perch, smiling all the while. He returned, loading the gun as he went.

"Alright! Let's see how you do. Remember how I showed you. Now, it's going to kick. So, hold on with both hands, and remember, the gun is an extension of you. You might feel like it wants to do what it wants, but you control it. Remember that."

Elise pointed the gun at the target, took a deep breath, held it and squeezed the trigger. The gun roared to life and flung her arms back toward her, but the tin can remained atop its perch.

Joshua laughed. "Try it again, but this time, try to remember to relax. Don't be so tense. Squeeze the trigger slowly and enjoy the moment.

Elise did as he asked, hit the side of the can and sent it cartwheeling off to her right. It felt amazing! The feeling was indescribable. She felt on top of the world. She felt empowered. She felt complete and uninhibited joy. She felt like spinning in circles or doing cartwheels but she did something even better. She lifted the gun and squeezed the trigger twice more. First one can and then the other flew off their perch and went rolling across the gravel.

"See! You're a natural!" Joshua said.

Elise lowered the gun and hugged Joshua.

"Thank you so much. I don't think I could ever repay you for this. This is awesome."

"You're very welcome my dear. I'm sure I could think of something," he said, and laughed.

She laughed at that, and they picked up the spent shells. Joshua put the gun in its case and then they went back up to the house.

CHAPTER ELEVEN

"This is very serious business and I wouldn't give it to you, if I didn't think you could handle it. It is for emergencies only. Keep it hidden and don't let anyone see it. If anything happens, I don't know you. Is that clear?" Joshua said.

He didn't really care what she did with it, but he had a pretty good idea what she would. He had to tell her that, because that is what she would expect him to say. He was after all, in the people business and he could certainly read people.

"Absolutely! I take this very seriously. No one will ever know. It will be our little secret," she said, whispering, as if to prove her point.

"Good. That's good. I hope that it brings you the peace that you desire. It's been with me for many years, and it has seen me through some tough times," he said, rubbing unconsciously at the scar on his temple.

Elise tucked the gun deep into her pocket, said her goodbyes and left. She walked home without looking over her shoulder once. The gun in her pocket assured her that she would be safe. Nothing bad could happen, while she was with it. She believed that with all her heart.

● ● ●

Joshua watched from the window as Elise walked happily down the street. He put on his hat and prepared to go up town. He had some errands to run and some people to see; after all, they were what made his world go 'round.

93

He waited until Elise was long gone from sight. It sure wouldn't be a good idea for her to see him talking to Abe, so he had to bide his time. Abe was right where he knew he would find him. Abe, apparently was drawn to the river as well, or maybe it's just that most people are, especially at times that they need its therapy. In any case, Abe could be found down by the river, on most days. He usually preferred to be farther down-stream from the dam, just to avoid running into anyone.

"Haven't seen you in a while. I'd ask you how things have been, but I guess that I already know the answer to that question. It's too bad the way this all worked out. I feel like I could have helped in some way. I know it isn't rational. It's just that, I don't like to see people in pain. You know? Anyway, I want to help, and I think that I've found the perfect solution," Joshua said.

"Yeah. What's that?" Abe asked.

"Well, it will take me a couple of days to get it organized, but I think that the results will speak for themselves. Can you meet me down in the little clearing, on the other side of the river? Oh, let's say six-thirty on Friday night. I'll explain everything then. I don't want to ruin the surprise, but it will be life changing! I can promise you that!" Joshua said.

"My life could certainly use some change, that's for sure. I'll be there. You going to give me any kind of idea, what you're up to?"

"Nope. Just trust me when I say, it'll be life changing. I'll see you then," Joshua said.

"See you then," Abe said, and went back to staring at the river.

Joshua got up and walked in the direction of his house. He still had some time to kill before the high school let out for the day, and there were still things to tend to at home. Besides, an idle mind is the Devil's playground he thought, throwing his head back and laughing. One down and two to go, he thought, whistling happily as he went.

• • •

Walt missed football practices after school. He enjoyed the practices as much as playing the games themselves. Their season was now over. They had lost 21-20 in the semi-final game. No doubt, it was a game that they would have won, if Abe would have played. No one even mentioned his name. Walt wasn't sure if that was just for his benefit or not, but he was pretty sure, that Abe was a topic that no one felt comfortable talking about. It was like he didn't exist any longer or at the very least, people were trying to forget that he did. Either way, Walt was sure glad that he never saw him. He wasn't sure how he would react, if he ever did. He didn't think that he would be able to beat him in a fight but he also didn't think that it would stop him from trying.

"How's it goin? Walt, right?" Joshua said.

"Huh? Oh yeah. Hey how's it going. You're the guy that helped me with my beer," Walt said.

His demeanor changed, when he remembered that the last time he had seen him was the night of the party.

"How'd you make out with your car?"

"Fine, just fine, thanks for asking. Listen, this isn't a chance encounter. I came here today because I wanted to talk to you. I don't mean to brag but I consider myself somewhat of a people person. I've met Elise a few times down by the river. She loves it there. It gives her peace. I go there to eat my lunches and quite often she'll be there. We've become friends of sorts. Anyway, she seems to be doing much better lately, but I feel that she just needs a little push, to get her over the hump," Joshua said.

"It's weird that Elise never mentioned you."

Joshua just smiled.

"So, what are you proposing?" Walt asked.

"I'm glad you asked," he said, smiling an impossibly large smile and rubbing his hands together in front of his mouth.

"There's a little clearing on the far side of the river. Do you know where I mean?"

"Yeah. I know the place very well. When we were younger, we built the tree fort that's there," Walt said.

"That's the place. Well, that's even better, you two have a history with the place. That's wonderful! I wanted to do something special for Elise. Every time I talk to her, she gushes about how wonderful you are and how much she loves you. It's quite cute, actually. I know that she wants to move past all this nasty business that she has had to deal with, and I thought that if I could assist in any small way, well, it would be my absolute pleasure. I'll take care of everything. It's going to be a surprise, so I don't want you tipping her off. All you have to do is show up. I'll arrange a nice romantic dinner for the two of you. Say, six thirty on Friday night? Oh, and the timing is everything. It has to be precisely six-thirty. No sooner or no later or you'll ruin the surprise. Okay?"

"I'll be there. Thank you so much, you're too kind."

"It's my pleasure. Like I said before. I'm in the people business. What can I say?" Joshua said and started to walk away.

"Six thirty on the dot. Don't be late, or early for that matter," he said sternly, and then smiled.

"I'll be there, and thanks again," Walt called after him.

Walt watched as Joshua walked away and he smiled to himself. What a nice man. The world could use more people like him.

• • •

Elise put the gun between her mattress and box-spring. She didn't want Walt to stumble upon it when he was over. She didn't want to have to explain it to him. This was one thing that she wanted to do for herself and she felt better now than before she had gotten the gun. She was still amazed by how kind Joshua had been to her. She liked him very much. The world could use more people like him, she thought.

Elise couldn't go more than a couple of hours without taking the gun out. As soon as she put it back in its hiding spot, she would start thinking about holding it again. She continued that way for the day, until Walt came over after school.

"What do you say we walk to your house. I need to get out and stretch my legs."

Elise left the gun under her bed, of course. She didn't want Walt to catch her with it, and figured that she would be safe with him. Surprisingly, while she was with him, the thought of the gun only crossed her mind a couple of times, because even though she loved the gun, she loved Walt more.

They went to Walt's house and just hung out. Elise had supper with him and his G-ma and then went up to his room. They cuddled and kissed a bit but that was about it. They both wanted to take it slowly. Neither of them wanted a repeat performance of what had happened the other night. They were both okay with that, because it was the closeness that they wanted, more than anything. Around ten or so, Walt walked her home and she went to bed that night feeling happy and content. They hadn't done anything special but she still really enjoyed the evening and couldn't wait to see him again.

She pulled the gun out, held it and stroked it for a while, but her thoughts kept returning to Walt. She smiled, stuffed it under her mattress, climbed in bed, and within minutes, fell into a restful sleep.

The next morning, she walked with Walt again, on the way to school. This time she had brought the gun with her because she would be going home alone. She walked down by the river and lie down on a large, flat rock, near the water's edge. It was just a little past nine and the sun was just starting to get warm. She enjoyed the warmth of the sun on her skin and the sound of the water rushing past. She stayed that way for a while, then got up and poked around the edge of the water, looking for crayfish and salamanders. There were always crayfish to find but you had to be here on just the right day to find salamanders. So, none today, but she still enjoyed the morning nevertheless. Her stomach started to rumble and she checked her watch. It was 11:45, no wonder she was hungry. She couldn't believe how the time had flown by. Time seems to fly when you're not checking over your shoulder every few seconds, she thought.

She made her way up the rocks, to the grass on top. There was about forty yards of grass between where the rocks started and the road. The rocks themselves were mostly light grey in colour and they sloped probably another thirty yards from there down to the water's edge. The dam itself was only fifteen feet above the river's surface but it could be loud at times, when the water level was high. Today it was flowing as it normally did, and so it was noticeable, but not overly loud.

"Hi there!" Joshua called out to her.

"Oh, hi! I didn't see you there," Elise said, as she walked toward him.

"Pull up a rock, won't you?" he said pointing at the rock next to where he was sitting.

Elise sat next to him facing the river as he was. He offered her some of his lunch. She was starving and she was tempted, but she lied and said that she wasn't hungry. It smelled delicious and her mouth watered thinking about it, but it wouldn't be fair. She could get something when she got home.

"So, I was talking to Walt," he said, his eyes twinkling mischievously.

"I didn't realize that you knew Walt," she said, sounding scared.

"He has arranged a nice surprise for you tonight. He has asked me to make sure that you are there," Joshua said, continuing with his thought and ignoring her response, then added.

"Don't worry! Your secret is safe with me. Actually, it's our little secret anyway. Isn't it? I never told him anything. Nothing to worry about, except getting yourself there tonight."

"For what? Where?" she asked.

"I can't tell you that. If I told you, then it wouldn't be a surprise, now would it?"

"I guess not, but you're not even going to give me a hint?"

"I can say that Walt wanted to do something special for you. That's all I'm willing to say. I'll swing by your place at around 6:25. Make sure that you're ready. It's kind of time sensitive, so we can't be late."

"It all sounds so mysterious. I can't wait to see what he has planned," Elise said.

"Hey, I put a lot of planning into this too," Joshua said,

pretending that his feelings were hurt.

"Sorry, you too," she said, and kissed him on the cheek.

"Well, I have to be going. I'll see you tonight," he said and started to walk away.

He stopped and came back.

"I trust that you have it with you, just to be safe? You can never be too careful," he said.

Elise patted her side, where the gun was hidden safely in the deep pocket of her sweater.

"That's good," he said, patted her on the shoulder and left.

She watched him drive away and then walked quickly home. She was starving and she had to get something to eat. She hurried to the kitchen and began pulling things out and putting them on the counter. When she had finished raiding the refrigerator, she turned to see what she had to work with. There was a jar of pickles, a chunk of cheese, a piece of chicken, a cookie and a whole grain bun. Certainly not a gourmet meal, but when you're hungry, anything that fills the hole will do. She got a knife, cut the bun and then cut a pickle in slices, as well as the cheese. She got some mayo from the refrigerator and spread it on one side of the bun. She closed it up and gobbled it down hungrily. She then devoured the chicken, followed by the cookie. She had eaten so quickly that she began to hiccup. She grabbed a glass and filled it with a cola and tried to drink it. There was still some food in her throat and the cola wouldn't go down. She began to cough and cough, until her wind pipe finally felt clear. She chuckled a bit at her binge eating episode and began to put everything back where it belonged. Her appetite wasn't completely satiated but it was good enough for now. She would get a small snack later.

Her first order of business was to put the gun back into its hiding place and then figure out what she was going to wear tonight. She was thinking a little short dress; something that would show off her nice long legs. She would have to wear a sweater over top, because it was starting to get very cool in the evenings, plus she had to have someplace to hide the gun. She contemplated just leaving it at home.

After all, she would be with Joshua and then with Walt, so no harm could possibly come to her. She wasn't sure why, but she had a nagging feeling that she should bring the gun along anyway. Better to be safe than sorry, she supposed; better to have it and not need it, than need it and not have it.

That was all well and good. She could think up any number of clichés, or rationalize it however she wanted to, but the real reason was, she didn't want to be away from it. She felt so much better when she was near it, and didn't see any real reason that she shouldn't be.

She stuffed the gun under the mattress and turned her attention to getting things in order for this evening. She wished that she had some sort of idea of what Walt had planned for them. She wasn't sure how to dress, but she really didn't see how she could go wrong with the little black dress idea. She could take it off easily enough if that's the direction that the evening took and she was beginning to hope that that's what would happen. She was pretty sure that she was ready, and she was excited just thinking about it.

She lay her dress on the bed and put her black high heels on the floor in front of them. She knew it wasn't practical to wear high heels, but she didn't care. It was important to her, to be as sexy as she could possibly be and she wasn't cutting any corners. There was still plenty of time, so she went and grabbed a small snack. She spent the rest of the afternoon, doing her nails, waxing, plucking her eyebrows, showering, that kind of thing. She wanted everything to be just right and she wanted to make sure that she had all the bases covered.

Chapter Twelve

Walt was a little late getting home from school, which annoyed him, but he had to stay late to catch up on some work that he had missed when he stayed home from school to be with Elise. He just wanted to get ready for whatever was in store for him and Elise. It was awfully nice for Joshua to go to the trouble of doing this for her. He knew that she deserved it. He also knew, that people were drawn to Elise. How could they not be? She was smart, funny, kind, and it certainly didn't hurt that she was beautiful. Walt couldn't wait to see her. He knew that whatever Joshua had planned, was really going to be something. He could just feel it.

Elise finished getting dressed and took one last look in the mirror, just to be sure.

"Oh yeah! That's hot!" she said to the mirror.

She made her way to the door and unconsciously felt her pocket to make sure that the gun was still there. She stopped at her dresser, sprayed a little perfume in the air and then walked through it and out into the hallway.

Joshua was already waiting out front. He was early and it was a good thing, because her Mom decided that this was a good time, to give her the third degree.

"I don't like this honey. Why didn't Walt just pick you up or come with him? Who is this guy anyway? It doesn't seem right. An older man coming to pick you up; I don't trust him. You of all people, I should think, would have trust issues," Sharon said.

"Just because you don't know him. I do, and I'm telling you he is as nice a person as you could ever meet," Elise said.

"Well, your Dad is going out to talk to him. You might not, but we have trust issues. If your Dad thinks he's okay, then you can go."

"Mom, you're so embarrassing! I have to go or I'm going to be late."

"Go on outside if you want, but you're not going anywhere, unless your Dad says it's okay."

"Hhaa," Elise exhaled in frustration and went out to the car, where her Dad was standing talking to Joshua.

Joshua took a cursory look at his watch and then looked at Elise. He lifted one eyebrow, which said everything that needed to be said.

She made her way to the other side of the car and got in.

"Okay, have fun honey. You have your cell with you, right?" Bill asked.

"Yes, Dad. I'll call when I get there."

"Okay, see you honey. Nice seeing you again," he said, shook Joshua's hand and stood watching as they drove out of sight.

"So? You think he's okay?" Sharon asked him, when he came back inside.

"Joshua? Oh sure, he's as straight an arrow as you'd ever find. I've run into him a few times. Real friendly sort. He was disgusted by what happened to Elise. I could tell that it bothered him when he talked about it," Bill said.

"Funny, I've never seen him around before," Sharon said.

• • •

"You shouldn't blame your parents for being too over-protective, after everything that's happened," Joshua said.

"I know. If my Mom knew that I had the gun, then maybe she would have felt better. Then again, it would just have her worrying about a whole new bunch of problems. It's better this way, I guess."

"Not to worry. I set your Dad's mind at ease and you can call them when we get there. Besides we're nearly there now," Joshua said.

Joshua pulled into the parking lot and shut off the car. Elise called her parents and then followed Joshua across the bridge. She could see a little table in the clearing. It was set up near the tree fort that they had built, several years earlier. She smiled at the thought of building it with their friends. She could see candle light flickering off the trees and the table, but little else. It was dusk and although it was still light, under the canopy of the trees it was just dark enough, that it was starting to get difficult to see.

"I'll just be over there. I don't want to disturb you two," Joshua said, pointing back toward the bridge.

"Okay," she said distractedly. She was still looking toward the candlelight. Still looking for a glimpse of Walt.

It wasn't what she saw, it was what she heard. She instinctively, pulled the gun from her pocket, and lifted it in front of her and continued. Her pulse quickened and her arms felt heavy. She gripped the gun tighter and that seemed to reassure her. She pressed forward. She scanned the ground in front of her looking for the source of the sound. There it was again. She lifted the gun. It had fallen slightly as she walked.

It sounded like heavy breathing and it sounded like Walt.

"Walt! This isn't funny. Come out where I can see you!" she called.

She lowered the gun a little. What am I doing? I shouldn't be pointing the gun into the darkness. What if it is Walt? she thought.

• • •

Walt got to the small clearing, right on time. He checked his watch and saw that it was now 6:29. Timed that nearly perfectly, he thought. There was a little table with two chairs set up to it. The table had a black and white checkered table cloth on top of it, and a single red rose in the middle. There were two small candles that were flickering from either side of the table. The light reflected off the trees overhead. It took a second for his eyes to adjust, when he looked away from their flames. Beside the table was a large picnic basket and there was another black and white checkered blanket, spread neatly on the ground, off to one side. Walt thought about checking inside the basket, but decided to wait for Elise and be surprised along with her. What a nice man Joshua was, he thought; to plan and arrange this all for the two of them. He was truly one in a million.

Walt sat down at the table and waited for Elise to show up. He watched as the tiny flames danced atop the candles and before long he heard the unmistakable sound of footsteps approaching. He looked up, smiling in anticipation, but his eyes hadn't quite adjusted yet. He shielded his eyes with his hand but that didn't help at all.

"Hey, asshole. What are you doing here?" he asked, from the darkness.

Walt could feel the hate in him rise, instantly. There was no question, whose voice it was.

"What are you doing here? Get the fuck out of here before I do something we're both going to regret!" Walt screamed at him.

"Make me, fuckhead," Abe said smugly.

Walt screamed, as he charged forward, wildly. He meant to tackle him to the ground, but Abe side-stepped him and stuck his leg out, sending him sprawling face first into the dirt. Walt jumped to his feet and spun around to face him. He was standing looking at him, a smug grin on his face. This infuriated him even more and he charged wildly again. This time when Walt got close enough, Abe brought his knee forward and caught Walt flush in the nose. Blood sprayed on Abe's pant leg and down the front of Walt's shirt. Abe spun and punched him hard in the side of the face. Walt fell over onto his back and lie there looking up, panting heavily, as Abe knelt with one knee on either side of Walt's waist. Abe sat down hard, putting all of his weight on Walt's mid-section. He could see the rage on Walt's face and it made him smile. He picked up a large rock from beside him and held it high over his head. He wanted to smash his brains in. He wasn't sure why he hated him so much, but he did and he wanted him dead. Maybe then, he and Elise could finally be together.

•   •   •

"Walt this isn't funny! Come out where I can see you," Elise said from the darkness, continuing to walk forward.

"Oh my God! Abe, no!" she yelled.

Abe looked at her and then down at Walt, then back at her. He couldn't for the life of him, remember how he had gotten to this point. He tried to speak but nothing came out. He started slowly lowering the rock.

Elise cocked the hammer back on the gun and kept it pointed at Abe. A small blue spark shot from the gun to her hand. Elise saw Abe beginning to bring the large rock down, meaning to smash Walt's head with it. Elise took a short breath, held it and squeezed the trigger. Abe fell over on his left side and the rock fell on his neck. Elise ran over to where Walt was struggling to get to his feet. He kicked Abe's legs off his and stood up. His eyes were wide with disbelief. Elise hugged him briefly and then turned her attention to Abe. She kicked the rock off his neck and turned his head with her foot so that he was facing her. His eyes were wide open and there was a large hole just above his left eye. There was the briefest moment of satisfaction, before the reality of what had happened began to set in. She turned back toward Walt, grabbed him and hugged him for all she was worth. Her legs were shaking and if it weren't for Walt holding her, she would have fallen to the ground. Walt took her over to where the table was, and helped her to sit down in a chair. He was still in shock himself. He couldn't believe what had just happened.

"Where did you get a gun from?"

"Gun?" she asked.

"I had better take that," Joshua said, plucking the gun from her hand.

"I heard a shot. Is everything alright?" he asked.

Neither Walt nor Elise answered him, but that was okay. He already knew the answer to his question anyway.

Walt held Elise's face in his hands. "Are you okay?" he asked.

She didn't respond. She just continued to look through him as if he wasn't there.

"Elise? Elise? Are you okay?" he yelled, frantically.

"Stop yelling. Why are you yelling at me?" she asked, and Walt could see that her eyes were starting to focus.

She looked at him and then at Abe's lifeless body, lying a few feet away and then back to Walt, with a puzzled look on her face.

"It's okay. Everything is going to be okay," he said and hugged her tightly.

Walt didn't know what else to say. What could he say? He knew that things weren't going to be alright, but that's the last thing in the world that he wanted her to hear right now. He sat holding her in his arms, while she cried loudly and he cried silently so that she wouldn't hear him and become more upset.

They remained that way until the police came and tore them apart and they went their separate ways; each of them to endure their own separate Hell.

CHAPTER THIRTEEN

"There's no one living at that address. That house has been deserted for months, ever since old lady Simpson died three months ago. Everything is covered in dust. It's clear that no one has been there for a while," the detective said.

"So how do you explain that my Mom, Dad and Walt all saw him as well?" Elise said.

"You want to know what I think? I think that all of you were in on it. I think that you were the one that pulled the trigger, but I think that you all planned this after he raped you. That's what I think. There's enough evidence to show exactly that. I think that unless you confess, that you're all going to be doing some time. Sure, they might not do as much time as you, but they'll do time. You can count on it. I feel bad for what's happened to you, I really do, but you can't take the law into your own hands. Listen, I've known you since you were a little girl. I don't like this situation one little bit, but I can assure you, that if you confess, things will go a lot easier for you. The judge will likely be a little lenient on you if you show him that you're a victim in all of this as well."

"I don't understand! He couldn't have just disappeared! He could straighten everything out. All you need to do is talk to Joshua," Elise said.

"Right now, all we have is what you've told us. No one else has heard of this guy, let alone knows him. You're going to have to do better than that."

Elise remained silent and let him continue.

"So, where did the gun go?"

"I don't know! I've already told you. I don't know, maybe Joshua took it. I don't know what happened to it," Elise barked.

"So, are you saying that this Joshua fellow is the one that shot Abe?"

"I'm not saying anything," Elise said, and crossed her arms in front of her chest and sat back in her chair.

"Okay, well, you get comfortable then, because you're in for a long night," the detective said, and left the room.

Elise put her head down on the desk in front of her and cried. She thought about Walt and what he must be going through as well; not to mention what her parents were going through. Where the Hell did Joshua get to? He could straighten all of this out in a heartbeat. All he had to do, was tell them that she had to shoot him, to save Walt. She had to shoot him to save Walt, right? She didn't secretly want him dead and used Walt as an excuse, did she? She was so confused. Why couldn't she remember the events of the evening? Everything seemed to be in a fog, like it was part of a movie that happened to someone else. She struggled to remember, but came away with only bits and pieces.

She remembered getting ready and talking to her parents before she left. She could remember getting the gun out of her pocket and then the next thing she remembered, was hugging Walt and looking over to see Abe lying dead on the ground beside them. She wasn't even sure that it was her that shot him. Could Walt have shot him, or maybe it was Joshua? Why couldn't she fuckin' remember?

• • •

"So, Walt, who shot Abe? Was it you or Elise?" the detective asked.

"I'm not saying anything, until I talk to a lawyer," Walt said.

"Was it Joshua? Elise keeps talking about a mysterious guy named Joshua, but so far, we haven't been able to locate him. Come on! You guys need to help me out here. You are both looking at time, if you don't come clean."

"Like I said before. I need to speak with a lawyer," Walt said.

The detective, whose name was Mitch, left without saying another word.

Mitch flung open the door. Elise lifted her head and looked at him, wiping the tears from her eyes as she did.

"Okay Elise looks like we're going to be letting you go. We just have to do some paper work and then you'll be free," Mitch said.

"For real? Why? What's changed? Did you find Joshua?"

"I shouldn't say anything, but what the Hell. Looks like we'll be charging Walt instead. We have to wait for results from the lab of course but from the looks of him, he was involved in a struggle with Abe. When we test the samples from under his finger nails, I think we'll find that they match Abe's DNA. We haven't found the gun yet, but even without it we have a very strong case. He certainly had motive and opportunity and once we get the DNA results, it will be pretty damning evidence," he said, with a grim look on his face.

"No! You can't! He didn't do anything wrong!" she blurted out.

Elise thought back to shooting the gun at the quarry and how wonderful that the gun had felt in her hands. She remembered holding it out in front of her, when she got to the clearing tonight. She couldn't remember pulling the trigger, but it had to have been her.

"It was me! I shot Abe! I shot Abe," she said.

"I know you did Elise. At least, I figured that you did. I can only imagine how hard this has been for you. I'm sorry, but you can't take the law into your own hands. I think the judge will take into account what you've been through, when he hands down a sentence. I can't promise anything of course, but I believe that this is your best chance for leniency. I'm going to go talk to Walt and then I'll be back," he said quietly, almost apologetically.

"Oh my God, Walt! Can you tell him that I love him, and not to worry about me? Tell him, that I'll be fine."

"I will," Mitch said.

• • •

"Okay, Walt. You're free to go. Elise confessed, so you can leave. Don't leave town though, okay? We may still need to talk to you again. And Walt? She said not to worry about her; she'll be fine and that she loves you."

Walt couldn't believe what he was hearing. Why would she say anything without a lawyer present? How could he not worry about her? She knew better than that. Worrying about her, is all that he would do.

"Can I see her?" Walt asked.

"No, I'm sorry Walt. There's no way that I can allow that."

CHAPTER FOURTEEN

Walt left the room, wandered down the hall and out to the front desk. An officer handed him his personal affects and then he passed through a set of double doors and out into a small waiting room. His head hurt and he was tired beyond belief. He was emotionally drained and he didn't know what to do next. He lifted his eyes from the floor and saw Elise's parents and his Grandma sitting together in the waiting room. When they saw him, they stood and Sharon ran to him and hugged him, nearly knocking him down in the process. Walt had to take a step back to steady himself. His Grandma and Bill weren't far behind and they joined in one large group hug, right there in the middle of the waiting room. Walt was emotionally spent. He broke down and cried, holding on to the three of them, to stop from slumping to the floor. No one said anything. Nothing needed to be said. There would be lots of questions later, but they would have to wait.

After a lot of tears and a lot of hugs, they all went their separate ways. Bill and Sharon went to their home and Walt went home with his Grandma.

Walt was in no mood to talk and his Grandma sensed that, so she let him be. Walt kept going over and over it in his mind. He couldn't believe that they had gotten to this point. He couldn't believe that Elise had a gun with her, let alone shot Abe with it. Where was Joshua now? He had been so helpful, and now when they needed him the most, he was nowhere to be found.

Walt thought of poor Elise, sitting in her jail cell. He wished so badly that he could be with her and comfort her. He shuddered to think of what the future held for them. She had confessed to Abe's murder. Was there any coming back from that now? He was lying on his bed, staring at the ceiling, still trying to make sense of it all, when his Grandma knocked on his door.

"Walt, honey. Can I come in?"

"Of course, G-ma. Come in."

She opened the door slowly and peeked her head in first, as if to test the waters, before committing all the way. She came in slowly and walked to the side of his bed. She was carrying a plate with a sandwich on it and a glass of cola. She set it on his night stand and then sat on the edge of his bed.

"I thought that you might be hungry. If you don't feel like talking that's okay, I understand," she said quietly, almost apologetically.

"Thanks for the sandwich, G- ma. I'm hungry but I'm not sure if I can eat. My stomach is flip-flopping all over the place. I'll try in a bit. I would like to talk, actually. If that's okay with you? It would be nice to hear another voice, instead of me talking to myself, going over and over things in my mind and getting nowhere."

"Well, I'm not so sure I can help, but I'll sure try. I can listen that's for sure and you never know, that might just be what you need right now."

"You know Elise would never hurt a fly. She thought that Abe was going to kill me. I'm sure of it. That's why she shot him. I never even knew that she had a gun. I think that she got it from Joshua but I never knew that she had it. This is such a mess. I sure hope that her parents can hire a good lawyer. I hope that there is something that can be done. The worst part is, I think that she confessed, so that I wouldn't get in trouble as well. What kind of person does that? What kind of person puts everyone else before themselves, when they know the severity of the situation? I love her so much, G-ma. I don't know how I could go on, if she was to end up in jail," Walt said, breaking into tears.

G-ma re-positioned herself on the bed, so that she was closer to him. She held him in her arms while he cried.

"There, there. Everything will work out just fine, you'll see. I know it all seems so hopeless now, but I promise you things will look brighter in the morning," she said.

Walt felt like he was six again and G-ma was comforting him after his dog Fritz had died. He had the same empty, sick feeling in the pit of his stomach, then, as he did now. His parents had gone away for the weekend, to some cabin up north. Walt was in the backyard and his Grandma was in the kitchen making supper. He was sitting on the picnic table and throwing a tennis ball across the yard. Fritz would run after it, happily barking and wagging his tail as he went, then bring it back and drop it at his feet. Walt repeated this over and over, waiting for him to get tired of it, but he never did. He repeated it with the same enthusiasm every time, as if it were the first.

Fritz was an ugly dog to be sure, but he was his dog and he loved him dearly. He looked like a dirty dust rag that had been covered in dust and lint. His hair was predominantly grey but there were patches of black and white as well. His coat wasn't uniform in length. It was long in areas and short in others. One eye was blue and the other was green. One ear stood straight up and the other flopped forward. He looked like he was smiling constantly, because of a severe under-bite. He was, however, a sweetheart. He was always eager to play, or cuddle if that's what Walt wanted to do. He was Walt's dog. There was absolutely no question where Fritz's loyalty lied. He and Walt were joined at the hip. The only one that Fritz even came close to liking as much as Walt, was Elise.

Fritz's other past time, aside from playing fetch, was chasing squirrels. Walt had just finished throwing the ball for the umpteenth time, when Fritz saw a squirrel in the corner of the yard. He went tearing after it, barking crazily as he did. The squirrel ducked under the fence and into the neighbour's yard. Fritz squeezed himself under the fence and took off after the squirrel. Walt went to the corner of the yard to yell at him, to come back, but it was no use. He was too intent on catching the squirrel, and didn't pay any attention to Walt.

Walt jumped the fence and ran after Fritz, who was now out of sight. He rounded the side of the house and looked down the driveway but Fritz was nowhere to be seen. He could hear him barking around the corner and down the street. Walt took off in the direction of Fritz's barking. A red Ford pick-up truck passed him and turned the corner. It had just gotten out of sight when he heard the squeal of rubber on the pavement as he slammed on his brakes. Walt had a sick feeling in his stomach as he rounded the corner. All his hopes that Fritz may have escaped were dashed. The elderly gentleman who was driving the pick-up was knelt at the front of his truck. He turned to look at Walt as he approached. Fritz was lying on his side, motionless, a few feet in front of the truck.

"I'm so sorry. I didn't see him until the last second. He ran out from behind that car," he said, pointing to the car parked beside him.

Walt didn't respond. He knew it wasn't his fault, but that didn't change the fact that his dog was dead. He scooped Fritz up and carried him to the curb and sat with him on his lap. Fritz was limp in his arms. Walt hugged him tightly and Fritz smiled back at him. He sat holding him for a few minutes and cried until Fritz's fur beneath his face was soaked. The elderly gentleman stood off to the side and waited patiently.

When Walt lifted his head, the elderly gentleman said: "I'm sorry son."

"It's not your fault Mister," Walt said, got up and walked back home, carrying Fritz in his arms.

G-ma met him at the front door.

"Oh, honey."

"He was chasing a squirrel and he ran out in front of a car," Walt said, through a fresh volley of tears.

"Come on, bring him into the back yard."

She opened the small gate at the side of the house and let him in. Walt walked through the gate and took Fritz to the back, where the garden was. He looked at the ball lying by the picnic table and began to cry even harder. He lay Fritz on the grass and knelt beside him. He stroked his uneven fur with the palm of his hand and talked to him. G-ma knelt beside him and put one arm around his shoulders and petted Fritz with the other.

"He was such a nice doggy. At least he didn't suffer. He didn't, did he?" G-ma asked.

"No. I heard the tires squeal and by the time I ran around the corner he was already dead. I think he was killed instantly. He looks like he's just sleeping. I wish he could wake up. I can't believe he's gone. A few minutes ago, he was barking and wagging his tail and I was playing fetch with him, and now he's gone," Walt said, bursting into tears again.

"There, there. I know, let it out," G-ma said, hugging him and running her free hand through his hair.

G-ma was doing the same thing right now. He hadn't thought of Fritz in a long time. G-ma was comforting him, and he was grateful for her attempt to make it better in some small way, but it didn't work then and it wasn't working now. There was nothing she could do to change the fact that Elise was in jail and there was a very real possibility, that she would be there for quite some time. It all felt like a bad nightmare. Unfortunately, he was wide awake and that didn't seem likely to change in the near future. There was absolutely no way that he was sleeping tonight.

"I appreciate everything that you're trying to do G-ma. I really do, but I think I'm going to go for a walk and try to clear my head. The thoughts keep going around and around, and they just won't stop. Sitting here doing nothing is going to drive me crazy and there's no way that I'm going to be able to sleep."

"I understand. Be careful please, and take your cell phone, just in case."

"I will. I just need to move. If I sit here, I'm going to go stir-crazy."

"'Okay, dear. Wake me when you come home, so I don't worry and dream bad dreams all night."

"I will," he said, and made his way to the door.

He couldn't wait to get out of there. He knew G-ma would worry the entire time he was gone, but it couldn't be helped right now. He walked quickly down the street in the direction of Elise's house. It wasn't a conscious decision, it's just the way he always walked. Why would tonight be any different? Why? Because Elise was sitting in a fucking jail cell and who knew when she was ever going to get out; that's why.

He slowed as he passed Elise's house. There were a good many lights on. Evidently Sharon and Bill weren't going to sleep tonight either. He knew it would probably help if he went to talk to them. They probably had a million questions, but he couldn't deal with that right now. He had to keep moving, he would go see them in the morning.

As he walked, he thought about the events of the night. He was glad that Abe was dead. Yeah that's right. He deserved what he got, but he wished that Elise hadn't been the one to do it. He wondered where Joshua had gotten to. He just disappeared into thin air. Hadn't he taken the gun from Elise's hand. Yeah, that's right. He showed up, took the gun and then disappeared again. He wished that he could find him and talk to him. He could really help Elise's case. He could tell them that she had to kill him; that, if she didn't, he was going to kill Walt. He'd be sure to tell them that, but would they believe him? He found it strange that they never came back in and asked him any more questions. Maybe he watched too many movies. He wasn't sure, what the normal procedure was.

He was now getting close to the river and he could see the blue and red lights from several police cruisers, that were still there. The entire clearing on the other side of the river was awash with white lights. He supposed that they were still searching for evidence. Well, they weren't going to find any gun, but they would find the rock that Abe had held over him, that he meant to brain him with. That should be enough to corroborate his and Elise's story of self- defense. He knew there was no way that he was going to get near the place and he wasn't sure that he wanted to anyway. He knew it was crazy but he just wanted to be close to Elise, so he went to the police station. They wouldn't let him see her of course, but it helped knowing that she was close by. He sat in a chair in the waiting room for a couple of hours, before he felt the need to get moving again.

•   •   •

Elise sat on the concrete bench, staring through the bars of her cell and into the next one. A scruffy, thin guy in his early twenties was sitting on a toilet in the middle of the cell. Elise looked away, when he lifted his head and looked at her.

"What are you in for?" he asked.

Elise put her head in her hands and began to cry softly.

"Don't feel much like talking? That's okay. Must be your first time, by the looks of you. I've been in and out of jail, most of my adult life. I don't know what they expect. I'm an addict, I told 'em that. They let me out, I ain't got no money, no job, so I steal to get money to buy drugs," he said.

Elise lifted her head, when she smelled cigarette smoke. She looked in his direction. He was hunched over, hiding his face from the camera in the corner of the room. He took a couple of quick hauls on his cigarette, snuffed it out and made his way back to the toilet. She wanted to look away, but found that she wasn't able to. She couldn't believe what she was seeing. He hiked his pants down around his knees, produced a small plastic bag, put his cigarette and a couple of matches in it, and shoved it into his anus. He did up his pants, stood up and smiled at her, before lying down on his own concrete bench.

"Don't look so surprised, you look like you've seen a ghost. Once you've been through the system a few times, you'd be surprised by what you are capable of," he said.

Elise didn't realize that she was still staring at him, and she quickly looked away, her cheeks flushing red.

"Yup, first timer for sure," he said, laughing.

Elise rolled onto her side, facing the wall, and began to cry again.

•   •   •

Joshua picked the gun out of Elise's hand and put it safely in his pocket. She hardly even noticed that he had taken it from her. He bent down and picked up the large rock and stuffed it under one arm and headed for his car. He had to keep shifting the rock from one arm to the other as it got too heavy. He made it to the bridge, then let it fall into the water below. He stood for a moment, enjoying the cool breeze in his face. He pulled out his pipe and stuffed a pinch of tobacco in it. He lit it, took a nice long haul on it and let it out slowly. Another night, another job well done, he thought. He walked slowly up the slope to his car. I'll be back, soon. Yes, I'll be back, he thought, as he drove out of town.

• • •

Walt wandered slowly home and was now sufficiently tired, to attempt getting some sleep. He woke his G-ma up as promised, said good night and then went to bed.

In the morning, when he awoke, he felt as though he had been run over by a large truck. Everything was achy and he was still unbelievably exhausted. He grabbed something to eat and went to see Elise's parents.

They were sitting at the kitchen table with their hands wrapped around their coffee mugs, their heads hanging. Sharon looked up when he came in. She was usually full of energy, but not this morning.

"Good morning Walt."

"Good morning," he said and sat down at the table, across from her.

Bill just nodded at him and he nodded back.

"Any word?" Walt asked.

"We talked to our lawyer last night. She's going to have a bail hearing tomorrow. He thinks that it's fifty-fifty, whether they let her out on bail or not. She isn't a threat to flee and she isn't a threat to the community, so she has that going for her. She did confess however, and that makes things more difficult. He said that he will argue that the confession was under duress and maybe the judge will buy it. We'll have to get a second mortgage on our house to post bail. He said, they will likely want fifty thousand," she said, and then put her face in her hands.

Bill reached over and grabbed her hand for comfort.

"What the Hell happened last night?" Bill asked.

Sharon removed her head from her hands and seemed to perk up a bit. It was a question that she was dying to have answered as well.

"Joshua set up a nice romantic dinner for the two of us, but Abe showed up, and we began to fight. I'm pretty sure, that if she hadn't shot him, I would be the one that would be dead right now. We need to find Joshua. He was there and saw it all, I think. I'm not sure how much he saw, actually. I think he's our best chance though and I think that he's the one that Elise got the gun from as well."

"I can't believe that she had a gun. I can't believe any of this is happening," Sharon said, putting her head in her hands, again.

There was a long silence after that. They were all so tired, and just thinking was a task that was too tiresome for them to endure. Walt got up to get himself a coffee, then sat back down. He didn't normally drink coffee, but he figured it couldn't hurt at this point. Finally, after several minutes had passed, he broke the silence.

"I was at the police station earlier and they wouldn't let me see her. It helped just knowing that she was close, though… I'm going to see if I can find Joshua. I don't know much about him, but I'll ask around and maybe someone can point me in the right direction. Take care. Call me if you hear anything, please."

Both just nodded in agreement, without saying a word.

Walt went out onto the front steps and stood, wondering which way to go. He had no idea where to start. Someone in town, had to know him. He walked toward downtown. Maybe he would get lucky and run into him, or maybe someone could tell him where he lived.

Walt came up empty. No one knew who he was talking about. It was as if he never existed. His only hope, was to run into him. He sat on a bench, right in the heart of downtown. He figured that if he sat there long enough, then eventually he would see him. He sat on that bench for four hours and nothing. He heard a lot of people talking about Elise. Most people that he overheard, thought that she was guilty, but most of them said that they didn't blame her. It didn't really make him feel any better. She was still in jail.

Discouraged, he dragged himself back home and went to lie down for a nap. Now, he was just trying to get through the day, waiting for tomorrow and Elise's bail hearing.

Two hours later, G-ma woke him up, because there were two policemen at the door. Walt went with them to the station, so that they could question him some more.

They got him to tell the story about what had happened the night before. He had already told it several times, so he wasn't sure why he was going over it again.

"Well, that's the same story you told us last night. Almost verbatim, actually. It's the exact same story that Elise has told us. Listen Walt, I've known you since you were a little gaffer, and Elise too. I want to help you guys, but unless you can come up with this Joshua fellow to corroborate your story, I'm not sure that there is much I can do. We looked all over the crime scene and there's no sign of the rock that you described. It's all open there, nothing but dead leaves and grass. If there was a large rock there like you described, we would have found it," Mitch said.

"I don't know what to tell you. It was there. I swear it was!"

"Okay, well, if you think of anything else, call me. In the meantime, we're going to keep an eye out for this Joshua fellow as well. I'm afraid that without him, Elise is in a whole heap of trouble."

They offered him a ride home, but he decided that walking was a better idea. He tried to remember what had happened to the rock after Elise had shot. It fell to the ground, obviously, but he couldn't remember seeing it after that. He was hugging Elise and never even noticed that Joshua had left. It was a good-sized rock. He couldn't for the life of him figure out why the investigators couldn't find it.

CHAPTER FIFTEEN

The next morning was the bail hearing. Walt had butterflies in his stomach. He was scared, anxious, nauseous, but he couldn't wait to see Elise.

He rode with his Grandma to the courthouse and they met Elise's parents out front. They hugged quickly and then went in. After a little confusion, they were directed to the appropriate area. None of them had ever stepped foot inside the court house before.

They went and sat down in one of the pews, all huddled together, near the front. The pews reminded Walt of the ones in church, only these ones were lighter in colour and spaced farther apart.

Before long, the courtroom was standing room only. Apparently, everyone wanted to catch a glimpse of the murderer. There were several reporters from the local newspaper and even one from a T.V. station, in the city. It was a zoo. The noise was deafening. People were talking and laughing. Laughing, yes laughing. Walt was furious. He wanted to stand up and yell at the top of his lungs for everyone to shut the Hell up, and show some fuckin' respect. One person was dead and another's life hung in the balance. Hell, the whole family's future hung in the balance, his included, and people were treating it like it was a fucking party.

The noise subsided and then ceased altogether. Walt knew that it could mean only one thing. He turned with everyone else, to see Elise being led into the courtroom. It reminded Walt of every wedding he had ever been to. It was the same reaction that people have when the bride enters the back of the church. Everyone stopped talking and turned in unison, toward the back of the room. Only this time it was no bride, it was Elise, his Elise, beautiful Elise.

She was wearing an orange set of coveralls. She had handcuffs on her wrists and there was a chain that ran from there to a chain that attached to cuffs around her ankles. She shuffled along, unable to take a full stride. A guard held on to her right arm and one held on to her left. They took her and put her in a small Lexan enclosure in the middle of the courtroom. There was a hole cut out in front for her to speak and hear through. The rest was solid, but see-through. She sat on the small pew inside, waiting for the judge to address her. She looked tired, really tired. Her hair was combed, but greasy. Her face was red and her eyes were puffy. Walt could tell that she had been crying and who could blame her. Her shoulders were slumped forward and her cracked lips were set in a tight grimace.

Walt tried to wave to her several times, but she didn't see him. Finally, she did see them and she offered up a half-hearted wave and tried to smile, but failed miserably. Her smile looked more like she was in pain and she was trying not to show it. Walt's heart sank when he saw her in this condition. He wanted to run to her and comfort her, but sadly he knew that he couldn't.

At the front of the room was an elevated platform that was five feet above the rest of the room. There were steps on either side to get up to this level. There was a single door, behind a huge desk and it was through this door, that the judge entered the courtroom. Elise's lawyer sat at a desk on the right side of the courtroom near the front and the district attorney sat at a desk on the left. In between the two of them was the stenographer.

"Please rise. Criminal court is now in session. Honourable Judge Jackson, presiding... Please be seated," the bailiff instructed.

The district attorney read out the charges against her and asked the court to deny her bail, based on the severity of the crime and the fact that she had confessed to it. Her lawyer countered with the argument that she wasn't a flight risk, she wasn't a danger to the community because it was an isolated incident, it was self-defense and her confession was obtained under duress.

The judge looked over some papers in front of him. He looked up at Elise for a long time maybe trying to assess how dangerous she was. Who knows what he was thinking? After several minutes without saying a word, he finally spoke.

"I'd like to hear from the defendant. Ms. Elise Marie Reid; I would like to hear from you. Why should this court grant you bail?"

"I didn't mean for this to happen. It only happened because I was protecting the life of someone I love. I would not leave town, because everyone I care for is here. I'm sorry. I didn't want for any of this to happen," she said, crying.

The judge paused for nearly five minutes. He shuffled papers around on his desk. He rubbed his temple with his thumb and removed his glasses, then put them back on. Walt could hear him exhale loudly, several times. He was clearly mulling over his decision very carefully.

Finally, he took off his glasses and set them aside. He looked sternly at Elise and then began to speak.

"It is the opinion of this court that this was an isolated incident. Further to that, it is my belief that Ms. Reid is not a flight risk. It is not the position of the court to decide at this time, if she is guilty or innocent. We are here to set bail. That being said, I set bail at fifty thousand dollars and order you to meet with a parole officer once a week until your preliminary hearing, to be set for two months from today," he said, got up from his desk and left the courtroom.

Elise turned to look at us. She smiled, only this time her smile was wide and genuine.

The guards led her out of the courtroom. The murmur of the crowd became very loud and the flashes from the reporters' cameras filled the room.

For now, the sick feeling in the pit of Walt's stomach was gone and he smiled for the first time since this ordeal had begun. He couldn't wait to see Elise and hold her again.

It took most of the day for all the paperwork to be filed, processed, and for Elise's parents to post bail. At 4 o'clock, Elise walked out of the courtroom, free for the time being. She was still wearing the same dress from the other night and carrying her heels in her hand. She ran to where Walt, G-ma and her parents stood waiting. They all joined in a long group hug and then shielded Elise from reporters, as they walked to her parents' car. Walt and G-ma followed them to her house and went in to visit for a while.

Elise was very tired and didn't feel much like visiting. She did the best she could, for as long as she could, but eventually she needed to go lie down for a nap.

"I didn't sleep much in the last couple of days, if at all. Would you mind, if I went to have a nap?" she asked.

"Of course, honey. We understand," Sharon said.

"And Mom, Dad, thanks. Also, I was wondering if it would be okay, if Walt stayed here with me?"

Sharon looked at Bill and he nodded back. Walt was pretty sure, that at that moment, they would grant her just about anything that she requested.

"If that's okay with you?" she asked, Walt.

"Absolutely," Walt responded.

Mostly because he wanted to be with her and never let her go, but he was also damn tired. The last couple of days had taken their toll on him as well, and he could sure use a nap.

"Is it alright if we just cuddle. We can talk later. I'm so tired and I just want to fall asleep in your arms," Elise said, when they got to her room.

"That's fine with me," he said and kissed her.

Walt lie on the bed beside her, spooning her. His right arm was beneath the pillow and his left arm was wrapped around her. She held his left hand with her right.

"I love you Walt."

"I love you, too."

He held her tightly, enjoying their closeness. He listened to the sound of her breathing, and it wasn't long before she had fallen asleep, and it wasn't long, before he joined her.

"Walt, are you awake?" Elise asked, quietly.

"Yeah, just waiting for you to wake up."

She rolled over, so that she was facing him.

"I'm so glad that you're here with me. I was so scared in jail and I thought that I might not get out. I'm terrified that I might still go to jail. I mean, I confessed to it, and if we can't find Joshua, then they are going to think that we planned this whole thing. I don't know how I would make it in jail. I was there for two days and I couldn't handle it. I can't do twenty-five years. We'll see what the lawyer says, but I think we're screwed," Elise said.

Walt thought the same thing; that if they couldn't find Joshua, then they were probably screwed, but he wasn't about to tell her that.

"We'll find him, don't worry. He's always popping up. He'll pop up again," Walt said.

"It's just that… I think that he may have taken off. It was his gun and he probably doesn't want to answer to why I had it."

"You're probably right. Why did you have his gun?"

"I didn't tell you because I didn't want to worry you. Then I didn't tell you because I loved the way it made me feel. It was like it made me feel stronger and less like a victim. I was down at the dam one day and Joshua was there eating his lunch. Abe came by and I freaked out. The next day I went to Joshua's and he showed me the gun. Then he let me shoot it in the old quarry behind his house. I know, I should have told you. I'm not really sure why I didn't…Walt, we should go check his house, maybe there's a clue as to where he went."

Walt looked at his watch. It was nearly ten o'clock and he was starving.

"Fine by me, I just want to swing by my place, get something to eat and check in with G-ma first."

"Sounds good. There's something else that I want to talk to you about. Let's go and I'll tell you on the way," Elise said.

They checked in with her parents quickly and then were on their way. They ate a quick snack at Walt's. G-ma was already sound asleep, so they let her be.

"I had a lot of time to think when I was in jail and I remembered something from when we were kids. It might be a coincidence, I don't know. It's going to sound a little off the wall but...Okay, so you remember the day your parents died? Of course you do, I'm sorry. That's not what I meant. Do you remember the dream that you had the night before?"

"No, I'm not even sure what you're talking about."

"Yeah, you had this incredibly vivid dream and it shook you up, a lot. You don't remember that?"

"No, I don't. Not at all."

"Wow, okay, so you dreamt that your parents were killed on their way to my house and that we had drifted apart."

"Really?"

"Yeah, and that's not the best part!"

"What do you mean? I don't remember any of this."

"Yeah, you were pretty weirded out about it. I made light of it at the time. I thought it must be a coincidence. I mean, what else could it be, right? I don't know why I never thought about this before, but I had a lot of time to think when I was in jail."

"That's incredible."

"You haven't heard the best part yet. You went on to say that you had met a guy in an alley and that he told you, that you could go back and do it over. Live your life again. Isn't that messed up?"

"Yeah, that's some messed up dream."

"It gets better. You had already begun to forget some of the details of the dream. You couldn't remember the guy's name, but you described him to me. You really don't remember any of this?" Elise asked, a puzzled look on her face.

"No, I don't remember any of this. You have my attention though. Go on."

"The man that you described, fit Joshua to a tee. It seems a little far-fetched I know, but what if...?"

"What if, what? What are you trying to say?" Walt asked.

"What if, it was the same guy?"

"I'm not following you? What do you mean, what if it was the same guy? The guy from my dream?"

Elise took a deep breath and let it out slowly and gathered her thoughts.

"I know it sounds crazy, but how did you know that your parents were going to die and on the exact day, no less? Explain that to me."

"I can't. What's the alternative, that I was re-incarnated or something?"

"I don't know, maybe it's all the stress that I've been under. I don't know, but I do know that it's awfully strange. I would just like to find Joshua. I have a few questions that I would like him to answer. Do you know, that all I can remember from the other night was meeting you, then hugging you, and when I looked over, Abe was already dead. At one point, I thought that you might have killed him. Doesn't that seem strange?"

"Yeah, it does, but I think that it might just be the stress of the situation, that's all."

"I just thought that it was strange that I couldn't remember and that you can't remember your dream either. Not only can you not remember the dream, but you can't remember telling me about it. Odd, that's all."

They kept walking in silence for a while, before reaching Joshua's house.

They went around back. The door was locked. They found a window that wasn't, they lifted it and went inside. There was a large row of cedars separating his house from the neighbour's house and there were several empty lots on the other side. Elise was confident, that no one would notice if they turned on the lights.

"If anyone comes, we'll just run out the back and into the quarry," she said.

The window that they crawled into was in one of the bedrooms. There was a single bed and a small night stand, but that was it. There was nothing in the drawer of the night stand and the bed looked like it hadn't been used. They walked out into the hall and then into the kitchen. Elise showed Walt where Joshua had gotten the gun out of the hutch. There was nothing in there now. The hutch and the table were covered in a fine layer of dust and there were no marks to indicate that anyone had been there recently.

"I don't understand. I was here a few days ago. It looked lived in then. Now it looks like no one has been here in months. If it wasn't for the hutch, I might think that I had the wrong place."

They checked all the kitchen cabinets and found nothing. The other two bedrooms were completely empty. They went into the back yard and followed the little path to the quarry. Elise turned on her little penlight so that they could see where they were going.

"I'll show you where he took me to shoot the gun," she said.

Walt followed her, down into the heart of the quarry. There was a large pile of gravel off to one side and that's where she was headed.

"I don't understand," she said, sweeping the floor of the quarry with her light.

"There were a lot of broken bottles here, and a bunch of tin cans that we shot, from there," she said, letting her light settle on a wooden frame that had only one bottle sitting on it now.

Elise swept the light in a big circle, trying to see if there was another wooden frame.

"This had to be the spot. I don't understand."

"Why don't we come back in the daylight? Maybe we'll find something then," Walt said.

"I guess," Elise said, shining her light at the solitary bottle one last time.

"What's that?" Walt asked, pointing at the bottle.

"A bottle," Elise said, kind of sarcastically.

"I know it's a bottle. I think there's something in the bottle," Walt said.

"Message in a bottle, maybe?" Elise said, managing a chuckle.

Walt held out his hand and she shook out the contents of the bottle. He unrolled the small piece of paper, that had a yellowed, weathered look, as if it had been there for quite some time.

Walt held it, while Elise shone the light on it.

It read: I'm sorry I couldn't stick around, but I'll be back. There would have been too many questions. Questions that I didn't want to answer. I'll make this right, I promise. After all, I am in the people business. Your friend, Joshua.

"Well, that doesn't give us much, but at least we can prove to the police that he's not a figment of our imaginations," Elise said.

"They might think that we wrote it."

"They can have it analyzed, if they want to. Maybe they can even get a fingerprint," Elise said.

Walt stuck the piece of paper back into the bottle for safe keeping and grabbed Elise's hand with his free hand. They walked back to his place, put the bottle up and then went into the kitchen to get some more to eat. They ate and then went into the living room to watch a movie. Before long Elise was asleep beside him. Walt text her Mom to tell her that she had fallen asleep. He sat with her, covered her with a blanket from the back of the couch and continued watching the movie.

Walt thought more about the dream that she had told him about. Then he started to think about the dream that he had had not too long ago. Holy shit! He thought. He looked down at Elise, sleeping comfortably beside him, just to make sure he hadn't said it out loud. He was in an alley, when he was older and there was a man there that handed him a gun. That man could have been Joshua. He never saw his face, but it very well could have been him. Now Walt could hardly wait for Elise to wake up. He was going to let her sleep. She had been through so much and he knew that she needed her rest, but he couldn't wait to tell her about his dream. At the time, it meant nothing to him, but now after hearing her story, everything had changed.

The mind is definitely a funny thing. Why he never thought of this earlier, was beyond him.

He continued watching the television, but he never really saw it. He couldn't stop thinking about what Elise had told him. He couldn't stop thinking about his most recent dream. What did it all mean and how did Joshua fit into all of this. He went over it in his mind. He couldn't remember any more details of the dream and he couldn't remember the dream that Elise had told him about at all. He was stuck in an endless loop. He wanted to talk to Elise, but he needed to talk to Joshua. He wanted to know what the fuck was going on and he was pretty sure, that he was the only one who could tell him.

Elise slept right through until the morning. Walt slept little bits here and there, but in the morning, he was exhausted. They ate breakfast and then went to the police station. On the way, Walt told Elise about the other dream that he had more recently.

"We really need to find Joshua. I want some answers," Elise said.

"That makes two of us."

Walt was still carrying the bottle with the note inside. He was nervous about losing the piece of paper or damaging it. When they got close to the steps of the police station, he shook the rolled-up piece of paper into Elise's hand. She unrolled it so that she could read it again. The white paper was a little yellow last night, but now it seemed darker, she was sure of it. She held the paper out and turned it over in her hands. She looked at Walt with a puzzled look on her face. She turned it back over and then over again.

"What the fuck is going on?" she asked, handing Walt the piece of paper.

Walt held the paper and looked at it and did the same as Elise. He turned it over and then over again.

"I don't understand. I know we didn't imagine it. We both couldn't have imagined it," Walt said.

Elise laughed nervously. "Well, we can give it to the police if I want to go with the insanity defense," she said.

"I don't get it. How can it be blank? Look at the paper as well. It's aged since last night. It wasn't this yellow," Walt said.

Elise took the piece of paper from Walt, stuffed it in her pocket and threw the bottle in the garbage.

"We really need to find Joshua, find out what the fuck is going on," Elise said.

"I looked all over town the last couple of days and no sign of him. I couldn't find one person that even knew him or had seen him. You don't know his last name, do you?" Walt asked.

"No, he never told me."

"Me either. So, we have nothing to go on."

"I know that he always eats lunch down by the dam. We could wait for him there," Elise said.

"Sure, why not."

They waited by the dam for an hour on either side of lunch time and nothing. They waited there for the next few days, and still nothing. They never saw him or his car. He seemed to have just vanished, as quickly as he had come.

In the meantime, Walt spent every minute with Elise. He had a friend get his schoolwork for him, but in all honesty, he never did any of it. He wanted to be with Elise, while he still could.

Elise met with her lawyer several times. He said that obviously, having Joshua's testimony would help a great deal. Without it, she was in big trouble. They didn't have a murder weapon, but a good lawyer would convince the jury that it wasn't needed. She confessed; that was the first strike against her. She was present when Abe was killed and she certainly had motive. Now, they might be looking at Walt, if it weren't for her confession. He was also there that night and he certainly had motive as well. They were going to try self-defense as motive, but without the rock and Joshua's testimony, it didn't look good.

Her lawyer said that the jurors would probably feel sorry for her, under the circumstances. That's what he was hoping for at least, but the judge would undoubtedly instruct them to consider the facts alone and not let emotions come into their decision.

Her lawyer said that her chances were probably less than fifty-fifty. The only good news, if you could call it good news, was that he really believed that she wouldn't serve more than ten years, tops. He said that there had been many cases, where a rape victim had murdered her assailant and the court and jury were more lenient, under the circumstances. It was certainly hard to consider that as good news at the moment.

CHAPTER SIXTEEN

Walt and Elise continued searching for Joshua, but they never turned up anything. Elise felt like she was living on borrowed time. Every week she went to see her parole officer and every week it brought her that much closer to her preliminary hearing.

Elise spent as much time with her parents and Walt as she could. She made love to Walt, every chance that she could get and it was wonderful. For a couple hours at a time, when they were together, she didn't think about what the future may hold for them. She was able to enjoy those stolen moments, unencumbered by the reality and the magnitude of her situation.

Walt felt it too. He was so happy to be spending this time with Elise. When he was with her, he was able to concentrate on her alone. It was the times that he was alone in his bedroom late at night that the reality of the situation loomed large in his mind. What would he do if she had to spend ten years or more in jail? Poor Elise, what would she do? He tried not to think about it, but he had to. He had to prepare himself for that real possibility. No matter what happened, no matter how bad it got, he was going to be there to support her. He would do anything for her. He would give his own life to protect her. He loved her that much. A life without Elise was no life at all.

Elise's preliminary hearing came and went, with no real surprises. Her trial wasn't scheduled to start until the spring, which was both good and bad. It gave them more time to find Joshua, but at this point, unless he just showed up, it was a lost cause. The good thing, was that Walt was able to spend more time with Elise, but they all seemed to be holding their breath, unable to move on, until this was behind them.

When Elise spent time with her parents, Walt expanded his search for Joshua to neighbouring towns, but the result was the same. Poof! He was gone. No sign of him.

Finally, Elise's trial started, and at the same time they couldn't believe that this day was already here. They were all nervous of course, but as you can imagine, Elise was a wreck. She wanted to get it over with by now, but she was of course, anxious about the outcome.

The trial went according to the script that Elise's lawyer had prepared her for. The D.A. tried to portray her as a vindictive, murderous monster, that had been planning Abe's murder since the beginning. Her lawyer tried to portray her as the victim in all of this. He tried to show that it was in self-defense, but that argument lacked substance, due to the absence of Joshua. Walt's testimony wasn't taken seriously because he was the boyfriend. The trial laboured on for nearly three weeks, before it was left in the hands of the jury to reach a decision.

They found her guilty of second degree murder and she was ultimately sentenced to fifteen years. Her lawyer said that she would be eligible for parole after serving half that time. All things considered, that was about the best that she could hope for, according to her lawyer. They thought, that the best that they could have hoped for, was for her to be found not guilty. They all knew that was unlikely to happen, but it still didn't prepare them for the moment that it became a reality. To think about something, and to have it become a reality, are two completely different animals. They believed that they were somewhat prepared, but nothing in this world could have prepared them, for when it actually happened.

Just like that, there was a huge void. A hole had been ripped through his heart and his life. Ever since he could remember, Elise had been there and now she was gone. Walt visited Elise's parents often. He needed their support as much they needed his. They would reminisce about times that they had shared with Elise. Later, when he got home, it would really hit him, when he was all alone. He thought about how terrible it must be for Elise. At least he had her parents to lean on. She had no one.

Joshua drove slowly down country roads. He had his window down, his arm resting on the door, enjoying the cool breeze. He inhaled deeply and let it out slowly. It was a good day to be alive. He had driven across the country and he had started a few more things in motion, that he had to check back in on. He had gone to visit Jason from the liquor store and he was right on track. Now it was time to get back to see how his favourite couple were making out. He figured that he had been gone long enough. He needed to wait for the right time. Timing was everything in these matters, matters of the heart. Now he was on his way back and he anticipated things would be ready for his return. He flicked on the radio and listened to it, whistling as he went. Yep, it was a good day to be alive, and the day was only going to get better.

•   •   •

The first Saturday that Walt went to visit her, they did more crying than talking. She was still in the county jail and was waiting to be transferred to the state prison. Walt arrived at five minutes to nine and was ushered into a small room, where he was patted down and then had to fill out a prisoner-visitor's form. When that was completed, they took him into another room. It was a small room with a glass partition down the middle. He was seated in a small chair and waited for Elise to be brought out. It looked just like it did in the movies. There was a phone that was hanging on a receiver to his right and a little shelf in front of him. Before long, Elise was brought into the room and she sat across from him. She managed a little smile, sat down and picked up the phone. She looked like she had lost weight already. Her hair was dull, her complexion looked grey and she looked exhausted. Walt nearly burst into tears from the sight of her, but he knew that he had to hold it together, for her sake.

Walt picked up the phone. He didn't know what to say. He wasn't going to tell her that everything was going to be okay. He wasn't going to ask her how she was. He knew how she was. He could see how she was, and that wasn't great. What could he possibly say.

"I love you," is what Walt said.

"I love you too," she said and began to cry.

Walt wanted so badly to comfort her, but he couldn't. There was a piece of glass an inch thick between them, that might as well have been a mile.

"I don't think I can do it. fifteen years of this; I don't think I can do it."

"Try not to think of that. Just take it one day at a time. One week at a time. Every week, I can come to visit. One week, one month, one year. It won't be easy, but we'll make it through it. Seven years is what you'll have to serve, then we'll have the rest of our lives to be together."

"I know you're right, but it's hard to think that way, when it's such a long way away. I've spent a week and a half in here and it seems like it's been a year."

"It will get easier. You'll fall into a routine, we both will. It'll get better. I promise. Hey, your parents are coming in a bit as well. They are excited to see you."

"Until they see me," she said, throwing her hands up.

"You're as beautiful as always."

"And you're a liar," she said, almost managing a smile.

They visited for a bit and it felt awkward. They couldn't wait until she was transferred to prison. Then they could sit together at a table instead of talking on a phone. They were still reeling from the newness of the situation and they hadn't completely come to terms with any of it.

When Walt left, he met her parents on the way in. He prepared them for what they were in store for. He didn't want Elise to pick up on any weird vibes from them. She had enough to deal with and she didn't need to be worrying about them.

Walt left the prison and went down by the dam to think. He sat at the water's edge for a while, enjoying the sound of the water spilling over the rocks. Before long, he began to get cold and he moved up the bank to where the sun was shining on a couple of large rocks. He reached out to touch the rock and felt that the sun had warmed it considerably. He lay down on the rock and closed his eyes. The rock warmed him from beneath and the sun's rays warmed him from the front. Through his eyelids, he could see the orange of the sun. He lie there for a while enjoying the warmth. A shadow crossed in front of him, he opened his eyes and squinted against the brightness of the sun. He shielded his eyes with his hand so that he could see what it was. He was in the process of sitting up, when a man spoke.

"If you don't mind me saying. You look like a man that's down on his luck."

Walt knew right away who it was. He would recognize that voice anywhere. He was furious, instantly. He sat up the rest of the way, and there was Joshua, sitting on the rock beside him, smiling at him.

"Where the fuck have you been? Elise is in jail because you weren't here to testify. Now you show up! It's a little late now. You can still make this right, she can appeal and you can testify at her new trial," Walt said, angrily.

"Easy, easy. Relax, I said that I would make it right, and I will. Remember? There's just no way that I could be linked to that gun. They would have taken it as evidence, and that's just not something that I was willing to allow. Come by my house later and we'll talk. Okay?"

"Your house? We were there and it was deserted. Where the fuck did you go?"

"Just come by my place later and we'll talk. Okay?" Joshua said, clasping him on the shoulder. A blue spark jumped from his hand to Walt's shoulder.

Walt jumped a little. "Still have that static electricity going on, I see. Okay, I'll be there. What time?"

"Oh...better make in nine o'clock."

"I'll see you then, and no bullshit," Walt said.

Joshua left and Walt continued to enjoy the warmth of the sun, lying on the rock. He couldn't believe that he had found Joshua. What a stroke of luck. A minute ago, he was furious with him, but he couldn't remember why. He wasn't sure why, but he trusted Joshua and he knew that he would make it all better somehow. He was happy to think that this nightmare could finally be put behind them.

Walt found himself counting the minutes until nine o'clock. The hands on the clock seemed to be stuck, but he watched them, just to be sure. The day dragged by at a snail's pace, but eventually it was time to go meet with Joshua.

He wondered what he had to say. How was he going to help Elise? He had no doubt whatsoever that he would help. He just wasn't sure at this point, how.

"Welcome my boy, welcome," Joshua said, as he opened the door.

Walt walked in and was greeted by the smell of fresh baked bread. It was nice and warm inside and the soft glow of lights coming from the kitchen, gave it a homey feel. He followed Joshua into the dining room and they sat down at the table. Walt looked at the many Knick knacks that adorned the hutch and the pictures that hung on the wall. A far cry from the last time that he was here.

"I think that we should get right down to business. You're probably thinking that you don't know anything about me. Well, I intend to remedy that. I'm going to tell you my story and then we'll get into what we are going to do about your little problem. Does that sound fair?" Joshua asked.

"Sounds good," Walt agreed.

Joshua told Walt the same story that he had, the first time that they met. Of course, as far as Walt knew, this was the first time that he was hearing it. It was a fascinating story and he hung on every word that he said. Joshua showed him the scars on his temples. Walt wondered why he hadn't noticed them before.

"That's an amazing story. If I had heard it from anyone else, I don't think that I would believe it, in a million years. I don't know what it is, but I trust you," Walt said.

"Well, it's the truth. They say that the truth shall set you free."

"So, what can we do about Elise?"

"Right! This isn't just about Elise. It's about you too."

"I know, but Elise is the one behind bars, at least I am free."

"Sure, you're free to wait around for the next fifteen years, until she gets out. What if I could offer you a way to set this all right again. What if Elise was never raped? What if she never went to jail? What if your parents had never been killed in that accident? How would that sound?"

"I would say that I would give anything for that to happen. But, that's not possible, is it?"

Joshua pointed at the scar on his temple.

"Anything is possible my boy, anything is possible."

He pushed his chair back from the table, stood up and turned around to face the hutch. He removed a small wooden box from the top drawer and placed it on the table. He spun it, so that the latch was facing Walt. He opened the latch and lifted the lid. Inside was a black, shiny revolver with a brilliant white handle, lying on a crushed velvet inlay.

"Go ahead, pick it up," Joshua urged him.

Walt reached forward and gingerly picked up the gun. A blue spark jumped from the gun to his fingertip, but he never noticed. He lifted the gun and felt the weight of it. It felt good in his hand. He turned it over in his hands, so he could examine every piece of it. It felt like it was part of him, familiar somehow. Walt looked at Joshua and raised his eyebrows, as if to say: "Okay now what?"

"I think you know. This whole mess can be fixed, quite easily. You know what you have to do."

Joshua was right. It was abundantly clear, crystal clear, what he had to do. He would do anything to spare Elise the pain of being raped and the heartache of going to jail.

Walt followed Joshua out the back of the house and down the small trail that led to the heart of the quarry. They stopped near the pile of gravel, where Elise had brought him, once before. There were shards of glass everywhere and two tin cans with bullet holes in them, perched atop the wooden frame. Walt barely noticed. He was so focused on the task at hand.

"I'll see you on the other side," Joshua said.

"See you on the other…" Walt said, and pulled the trigger.

Joshua bent down and deftly plucked the gun from Walt's hand. He lay his hand on his shoulder and then turned and walked away. The shards of glass shimmered in the moonlight from the otherwise empty, quarry floor.

CHAPTER SEVENTEEN

Walt awoke to the smell of sausages and maple syrup. He jumped from his bed and ran out into the kitchen. He flung his arms around his Mom's waist and hugged her tightly.

"What's gotten into you this morning?" his Mom said.

"Just had a bad dream that's all," Walt said.

"Well, the good thing about it is, it's behind you now and nothing but good things to come," she said, happily.

"Good morning, Walt," his Dad said.

"Good morning, Dad."

Walt ate his breakfast, like it was his last meal. He wanted to go see Elise. He had to go see Elise.

"Whoa, what's the hurry?" his Dad asked.

"I have to go see Elise."

"She'll be there, when you're done your breakfast," his Mom said.

Walt drank his juice and then put his glass and his plate, along with his fork and knife, in the sink. He ran to his room, got dressed and then said goodbye to his parents as he ran through the house and out the door.

"What's the hurry?" his Dad called after him, but Walt was already gone.

"I wonder what has gotten into him," he said.

Walt pedaled his bike as fast as his little legs would go and he was there in record time.

He opened the door and walked in. Elise's parents were sitting at the kitchen table, reading the paper and having their morning coffee and toast.

"Good morning," he said as he walked by.

"Good morning Walt. How's it…" Sharon said.

"That's not like him. I wonder what's up?" Sharon asked Bill.

Walt found Elise in her room, reading a book.

"Hey Walt. What's up?" she said, closing her book.

Walt sat on the bed and turned so that he was facing her.

"You look so serious," she said, laughing.

Her smile faded, when she realized that there really was something up, and that it did look serious.

"I just had something amazing happen to me. I think it may have been real. You're going to think I'm crazy, but I don't think it was a dream. It was far too real for it to be a dream."

Elise sat forward on her bed. Walt had definitely gotten her attention.

"Go on," she said.

Walt told her everything and then waited for her to respond.

"Well! What do you think?"

"Come on Walt! It had to be a dream," followed by: "We had sex!"

"Is that really the most important part of the story. Really?"

"It's kind of right up there! Yeah!" she said.

"Okay, never mind all that other stuff. I'm scared that my parents are going to die. Just humour me okay? I'll tell your parents that my parents can't come tonight, that they'll have to reschedule. I'll tell them that they went out of town. Then I'll tell my parents the same thing. Can you just go along with me on this?"

"Sure. If it's that important to you. So… we had sex?" she asked, raising an eyebrow.

"Yes, we did and I was amazing. Now, can we please focus on something else?"

"So, why was I in jail, in this dream of yours?"

Walt thought about correcting her and telling her that it wasn't a dream, but thought better of it. He didn't know what it was. He guessed that it could have been a dream, after all.

"You killed Abe."

"Why would I kill Abe. I don't really even know the kid."

"Let's just say, that when he gets older, he's not a very nice person."

"Okay, note to future self, stay away from Abe. Got it."

"So, you believe me?"

"Of course I do."

"You do?"

"Yeah, I believe that you had an incredibly realistic dream, in which we had sex," she said and then began laughing and tickling him.

Walt laughed like crazy and squirmed trying to get away. He was always a sucker for being tickled. When she had finished tickling him, he lie back on her bed, panting, trying to catch his breath.

"I'm going to talk to your parents. You want to hang out later?" Walt asked.

"Sure."

Walt went downstairs and talked to her parents. They bought it, hook line and sinker. He had never lied to them before and there was no reason for them to think that he wasn't being honest with them now.

When he got home, he told his parents the same bogus story. He hung around the house for a while and spent time with his parents and G-ma. Wow, did she ever look young.

Walt met Elise down at the dam and they did their usual thing. Playing by the water's edge. Looking for crayfish under rocks. Sitting on the rocks and talking. All pretty normal stuff, really. Before too long, Walt was anxious to get back home though. He wanted to make sure that his parents stayed home and he wanted to be there to ensure that it happened.

When he got home, his parents were still there. His Dad was out tinkering in the garage and his Mom was sitting at the table, reading a recipe book.

"What's for supper?" Walt said, referring to the cook book in her hand.

"You'll have to ask G-ma. Your Dad and I are going out for supper. We figured, we were supposed to go to Sharon and Bill's for supper anyway, so we might as well go out."

Walt felt like he had been kicked in the stomach. He didn't know what to say. He needed time to think, time to come up with a plan.

"Are you feeling okay? You look like you're coming down with something.

There it was. That was his in. They couldn't possibly go, if he was sick, could they?

"No, I'm not feeling well. I think you and Dad should stay home tonight, just in case I get worse," Walt said.

"Don't be dramatic; you'll be fine. Besides, G-ma will be here to look after you."

"Okay, I'm going to be honest with you. I lied to you and I lied to Elise's parents. I'm sorry. I had the most incredible dream last night. It felt more like I was looking into the future and the past at the same time. Either way, it felt so real that I am a little weirded out about it, a lot, actually. I dreamt that you and Dad got killed in a car accident tonight. I don't want you to go tonight. What can it hurt, if you just stay home? We'll never know if it was just a crazy dream, but at least you'll still be alive," Walt said, looking as sad as he could.

"Alright, you win. How can I argue with that kind of logic? If it will make you feel better, we can stay home. Maybe we'll order in some Chinese or a couple of pizzas. We can have a family night."

"Thanks, Mom. You don't know how much it means to me."

"You're welcome, besides, I'm too young to die," she said, chuckling a little.

Walt went to his room and played video games and read a bit of a book that Elise had given him. It seemed that most of the books he read lately, were ones that Elise had already read. That was good in one respect. Elise had the same taste in books as he did, so he knew that he would enjoy them. The only problem, was that he couldn't just read them at his own pace. Elise would continually bug him, asking him if he read it, how much had he read, what did he think? Sometimes, like today, he found himself reading, not because he wanted to, but because he wanted to keep her off his back. She could be such a pain sometimes. He really liked her.

Walt closed the book after having read only one chapter. He lie there thinking about his dream. The dream, that seemed to have been in HD earlier, now seemed to be in regular 720 or worse, and a little fuzzy around the edges. He could still remember most of the dream, but it didn't seem quite as real or important as it did when he first woke up. Dreams have a way of doing that, he figured.

He was beginning to get hungry, so he looked over at the clock on his nightstand. It was 4 o'clock and they usually didn't eat until 6, but he thought that he would go downstairs and see if he couldn't hurry things along a little.

His Mom was just putting the dishes away, that she had just taken out of the dishwasher.

"Hey Mom, can Elise come over for supper? Also, I was wondering if we could eat a little earlier than normal. I'm starving."

"Yes, to both questions. I'm hungry too. Go ask your Dad and see what he says. I could eat as soon as food gets here. Oh, and ask him if he wants Chinese or pizza?"

"Will do."

Walt called Elise and invited her for supper, then went out to the garage and found that his Dad was still puttering around in there. He had been busy. All the tools that had been lying on his work bench, were all neatly put away. The floor of the garage was clean and everything was put up on the shelves, where they belonged.

"Wow, you've been busy."

"Sure have. I even changed the oil in your Mom's car and fixed the weed eater that gave me fits all last summer. She's good to go for this year, now."

"Mom says that she's hungry. She wants to know if you want Chinese or pizza."

"I thought that we were going out for supper?"

"Change of plans, family night."

"Whatever you guys want, is fine with me then."

"Okay."

Walt went back inside and told his Mom that Dad didn't care.

"Okay, so what do you feel like having?"

Walt couldn't decide. Pizza and Chinese food were his two favourite foods in the world. He thought about it for a second. He knew that his Mom liked them both equally. He did know, however, that Elise liked pizza better.

"I feel like having pizza tonight," Walt said.

"Good choice. I'll order it right away."

A few minutes later Elise showed up and the pizza wasn't far behind. Mom made a Caesar salad to go with it and they all sat down to eat. Afterwards, they watched a couple of movies and had popcorn. Grandma made it through the first movie, but she was sound asleep and snoring, before the second one started. Dad had to turn up the volume on the T.V. twice, so that they could hear it.

That night, after Elise had gone home and everyone was safely tucked in bed, Walt had time to reflect on the day. He would never know if his parents would have died, if he hadn't intervened, but he was glad that he would never have to find out.

In the morning when he woke up, he could hear his parents talking in the kitchen. He couldn't hear what they were saying, and he didn't care. They were alive, and that was all that mattered. The terrible sense of foreboding that had plagued him the day before was gone and he never gave it another thought.

A week later, he barely remembered his dream at all. He knew that it had been incredibly life-like, but the details escaped him. It didn't much matter at this point, anyway.

He did have a recurring dream, that started soon afterward and continued for many years. He would have the same dream nearly every month and it was always the same. It was night time in his dream. The location changed from an alley to what looked like a gravel parking lot, but the dream itself was always the same. A well-dressed black man, would tell him that he looked like a person that was down on his luck, and then hand him a gun. He would say that he would see him on the other side, and then he would wake up. He didn't know the man; he had never seen him before in his life.

Walt's parents had never seen the man before either. Not before tonight, that is.

CHAPTER EIGHTEEN

Two months had passed since Walt had convinced his parents to stay home and order pizza; so, when they told him that they were going to Sharon's for supper, he never gave it another thought.

Elise was coming over and they were going to order a pizza. G-ma was watching one of her shows and she had already made herself a grilled cheese sandwich. So, they would have it all to themselves.

They wasted no time ordering it. As soon as his parents closed the door, Walt was on the phone. Fifteen minutes later, the pizza showed up at the door, and fifteen minutes after that, they were lying on his bed, trying to recover from having eaten too much. Walt turned on the T.V and they were watching some nature show. Walt was lying on his back and she had her head on his chest. Her hair smelled wonderful and the warmth of her body against his was nice. It happened slowly, nearly imperceptible at first, but there was no denying it. He re-positioned himself, hoping to hide it, hoping that she wouldn't notice. She moved when he did, and now she was no longer looking at the T.V. Her face was now facing his and she had her eyes closed. Good! She hadn't noticed. What a relief! He would have been so embarrassed if she would have seen; he didn't know what he would have done.

Walt could feel Elise's warm breath on his chin and lips, which wasn't helping matters. He tried to just watch the T.V. and not think about it. He managed to do just that... for all of two minutes, and then there was no use. He could think of nothing else. He thought about getting up and going to the bathroom, but he didn't want to disturb her. She re-positioned herself. Walt looked down at her and she still had her eyes closed. Her lips were now nearly touching his. He thought about closing his eyes and kissing her and just pretending that he was sleeping. Elise moved again and this time her hand slid from his stomach and came to rest on top of his erect penis. That was it! He couldn't take it any longer. He squirmed free from underneath of her and went quietly to the bathroom. Elise didn't move, she was sound asleep. Good, he didn't want to wake her. He went pee, after his hard on subsided, and then used a wad of toilet paper to dab at the wet spot on the inside of his underwear. He went back to his bed and slipped back underneath her, being careful not to wake her. No sooner did he get settled and she moved again. Her lips were nearly touching his again. He closed his eyes and tried to think of something else.

Elise leaned forward and kissed him. He must have jumped a little, because it scared him. He opened his eyes and Elise was looking at him smiling from ear to ear.

"I wasn't sleeping, silly. I was awake the whole time," she said.

"Real funny."

"I thought so," she said laughing.

"Whatcha got there?" she asked, pointing to his hard on.

Walt bunched the covers in front of him, hiding it from her.

"What's the matter? You shy?" she said, teasing him.

Walt could feel his cheeks turning red, and the more he tried to act like he wasn't embarrassed, the redder they got. He turned his head away from her, so that she wouldn't see.

Blue and red lights were flashing off the tree in the front yard and in through his window. He got up and made his way across the room, to look out. Before he made it, there was a knock at the door. Walt peered out the window and saw two police cruisers in front of the house. One was parked on the street and one was parked in the driveway.

He and Elise jumped from the bed and headed down the hall, toward the front door. G-ma was struggling to get out of her chair and was having a difficult time. They hurried past her, neither of them even thought about helping her. They were anxious to get to the door, to see what was up. Neither of them were prepared for what they were about to hear.

They heard the words, but they couldn't understand what they meant. They were shocked, they were stunned. There had to be some sort of mistake. They couldn't be right, could they? There must be some other explanation; there had to be. Walt reached out an arm to steady G-ma and Elise grabbed her other arm. All three of them stood, unblinking, looking at the officers.

The second officer repeated what the first officer had just said, as if they hadn't heard it the first time.

"I'm sorry to be the bearer of bad news, but your parents were involved in a motor vehicle accident. They were both killed instantly. I'm sorry," he said.

G-ma nearly fell, but Elise and Walt enveloped her in a hug that held her on her feet.

"Thank you," she said to the officer, then closed the door in his face.

The three of them went and sat down on the couch. G-ma continued crying. Walt and Elise were too stunned to cry. They just sat looking straight ahead. It took a long time before any of it sank in. Walt was numb. He felt like he should be feeling more emotion, given the tragic news that he was just presented with, but he didn't feel anything, just empty.

Elise stayed the night, and it was a long night. The longest night of his life.

Walt could remember only snippets from his dream but Elise filled in the rest. What the Hell was going on? How could he know that they were going to die? Okay sure, they didn't die the night of Sharon's party, because it never happened, but nevertheless they did die in a car accident.

•　•　•

Joshua looked at his watch. He was running late and he had better get moving if he was going to get there in time. Seems like old times, he thought to himself and chuckled. It was overcast, so there were no stars lighting the night sky. The moon was hidden behind the clouds and the night was an inky black. Perfect night for a walk.

Joshua pulled into a small lane way, shut off the car and got out. He walked out to the road, turned and went back to the car. Better pull in a little farther, just to be sure, he thought. This time when he got to the road, he was satisfied and so he continued walking. He walked until he was at a section of the road that was lined by trees on both sides. This spot would do perfectly, he thought. He loaded his pipe, lit it, took a nice long haul and then let it out slowly. He never tired with how wonderful, how calming it was to smoke his pipe. He only smoked it on special occasions, and this was certainly a special occasion.

He stood patiently at the side of the road. He hadn't needed to hurry after all. Oh well, better to be safe than sorry. He finished smoking his pipe, knocked out the ashes with the palm of his hand and put the pipe back in his pocket. He had best be getting ready; it was nearly time.

He could see headlights coming around the bend, just past where he had parked the car. He waited in the shadows at the side of the road, waiting for the right time. He stepped quickly onto the roadway and then took another step, so that he was right in the middle of the lane. The car was still far enough away to avoid him. He took two more steps forward and now he was standing on the yellow line. The car careened wildly to his right, flew off the roadway and straight into a tree. The sound was deafening. The sound of screeching tires, crumpling metal and breaking glass, followed by the hissing of steam escaping the radiator, were all music to his ears.

He walked over to the side of the car. She was lying crumpled at the base of a tree, nearly ten yards away. He was still gripping the steering wheel. Blood was pouring out of his mouth and nose. He mouthed the words, "help me." Joshua turned, walked back up onto the roadway and back toward his car.

Another night, another job well done, he thought and continued walking, whistling as he went.

Walt had been here before, twice before in fact. He didn't know that, however. All he knew was that his parents were dead and he had to move on. His G-ma was a tremendous source of support, as was Elise. He never could have made it through the next few weeks and months, without them.

Elise and Walt shared a bond that was stronger than anything, and Walt knew that nothing or no one could ever come between them. They spent even more time together now, since his parents' passing. G-ma watched her shows all the time. He would see her at breakfast time and would eat supper with her, but any free time he had, was spent with Elise.

As they got older, Walt couldn't help but notice how beautiful that Elise had become. He wasn't the only one. Everyone noticed it. She became the captain of the cheerleading squad in her sophomore year of high school. The same year that Walt started playing football.

One person in particular, really took notice of Elise's good looks. Abe, the captain of the football team. He asked her out several times, but she always turned him down. Walt was sure that she would say yes. After all, he was the captain of the football team and she was the captain of the cheerleading squad. It was a good match, right? Walt must have been a little slow, because he never figured it out. Sure, he and Elise hung around all the time and they even messed around a little bit once in a while. He thought Elise was too beautiful to be interested in him. Walt sold himself short. He was a good looking young man in his own right.

He always thought about what it would be like to be Elise's boyfriend and not just a friend, but he never acted on it. He was happy being her friend and being close to her and he didn't want to screw it up.

He dreamt about her at night too. It's not what you think! Okay, sure he did have a few sexual fantasies about her. What teenage boy wouldn't? No, his dreams were of a different nature. He still had the same recurring dream, that he had had since he was a kid. That dream never went away, it just became less frequent. In the beginning, he would have it every week, but now he only had it once every couple of months. It was still the same. A well-dressed man would hand him a gun, after telling him that he looked like a man that was down on his luck and that he would see him on the other side. Walt just realized that the last few dreams had been different. It was subtle, but different all the same. When the dream took place in a gravel parking lot, there were shards of glass, all around his feet. He still couldn't see the man's face, but he saw his hand clearer, and he had black skin. Walt wondered what it all meant. He had been having the same dream for many years. That in itself was strange, but now it had changed a bit, after all of this time. Weird.

The other dream he had was of him going to a jail to visit Elise. He didn't know where the jail was, or why she was there. The dream would start with him already being at the jail, waiting to talk to Elise and then somehow, he would be outside, searching, searching. He would spend the rest of the night looking for something and never finding it. He had no idea what he was looking for, he only knew that it was important that he find it. He would wake up exhausted, as if he had actually spent the night scouring the town, looking for whatever it was he needed to find.

He and Elise talked about his dreams, many times over the years, in fact. She even tried to get him to go see a hypnotist, but he never went. No reason really, he just never got around to going.

Walt never had a girlfriend. In the back of his mind, he guessed that he was secretly hoping, that one day he and Elise would hook up. It was strange, because Elise could have had anyone that she wanted and yet she never had a boyfriend either.

One day, Walt decided to ask her about it.

"You're kidding, right? You have no idea what my feelings are for you?" Elise said.

Walt couldn't tell if she was mad at him for asking. He had never seen her react this way before and he didn't know how to read her.

"I don't know! I'm sorry. I didn't mean anything by it," Walt said.

"Walt, I love you, but sometimes you can be so dumb. It's infuriating," she said, grabbed him and kissed him.

"I love you Walt. Don't you know that? I don't mean as a friend. I mean I want to grab you and fuck the shit out of you. That's how I love you. I know it's not exactly lady-like and I don't care. There I said it, I want to fuck the shit out of you. What do you have to say to that?"

"Okay?" Walt said, meekly.

"Good enough! Let's go to your place, my parents are home and your G-ma won't leave the couch, so I think we're safe," she said, grabbing his hand and walking toward his house.

Walt couldn't believe that this was happening. This was every teenage boy's dream. She just took charge and he was going along for the ride. He didn't want to ruin the moment, but at the time his mind betrayed him. He thought too much sometimes. That's just who he was and he couldn't help it.

"Are you sure about this. I mean, don't get me wrong, I really, really want to have sex with you, but I don't want it to get weird afterwards, you know? I wouldn't want to wreck our friendship, because that's the most important thing to me," he said.

"Which one of us is the girl here? You're not supposed to think of things like that. That's supposed to be a girl thing... I'm just playing. I've thought about it and I know that we can be both friends and lovers. We know each other better than anyone. I know that we'll be fine. Listen, I know what I said earlier was out of character and I hope it didn't turn you off, but I've been waiting for this for a while and I really don't think I can wait any longer. Well, I could, but I don't want to," she said, showing a little evil grin.

That seemed to do it. That's all he needed to hear; he was completely onboard now. No more stupid thoughts or stupid questions. It was time to live in the moment.

"Umm...Do you have protection?" he asked.

"At home I do. You mean you don't have any? I just figured every teenage boy in the country would have a rubber stashed somewhere."

"Well, not this one, sorry."

"It's fine, no big deal. We'll just have to swing by my place and then continue on to your place."

That was the beginning of it. A monster was created that day. Walt and Elise went back to his place, G-ma was watching T.V. as usual and they went to his bedroom and they weren't disturbed. Elise didn't fuck the shit out of him as promised, but they did make love and it was incredible. It wasn't awkward, like a lot of first times are. Walt could thank Elise for that. If it was left up to him, it would have been awkward as Hell. Elise helped him through it and it turned out very well. She was very good at communicating to him what she needed and he was eager to please her.

Elise couldn't get enough. Any time that they could steal away for a few minutes, or that her parents weren't home, or that G-ma was pre-occupied, Elise wanted to have sex. Walt certainly wasn't complaining, but on some level, he hoped that she would slow down, after the newness of it wore off. He missed the long conversations that they used to have and all the things that they used to do together. Now, all they did was have sex. He knew that anyone would be happy to be in shoes. Maybe it was just him thinking too much again. He decided to just enjoy the ride and let things work themselves out, which they did.

It lasted for a couple of months and then they started doing other things, like Walt had hoped. Now, he felt so much closer to Elise than he could have ever imagined. He thought that they were close before, but he never imagined that it could be like this. Their emotional bond had become so much stronger. The love that they now shared was so much deeper. He would rather die than see Elise hurt. He would gladly give his life to protect her.

CHAPTER NINETEEN

Walt made a huge error in judgement, of course he didn't know it at the time. When he told Elise about the amazing dream that he had, just before his parents' deaths, he left out one critical detail. He told her that she was in jail for killing Abe, but he never told her why, or when it happened. The dream, for him, had faded a long time ago and he didn't remember it at all. Had he told her the full dream, then maybe it would have changed things, who knows?

Well, he hadn't, and there was no reason to believe that the party on Friday night, was going to be anything but a great time.

Everyone was going. The entire high school would be there. The thing about their high school was, that everyone seemed to get along. There were different groups that were very noticeable at school, but no one group was singled out. It was a very progressive school. It usually meant that big parties were a lot of fun, without the usual fights that came when different groups clashed.

Walt and Elise decided to go together, of course. Elise's friends, Ashley and Hailey, wanted her to go with them, but she wanted to go with Walt. Besides, it wasn't like she wouldn't see them.

They decided to ride their bikes there. That way, they wouldn't have to worry about drinking and driving afterwards. It was a bit of a ride, but it was a nice night, so what the heck.

Walt threw a bunch of beers in his back pack and a few coolers in there for Elise and they were on their way. Someone would have a cooler with ice in it, that they would be able to use.

It was a nice ride. The night was clear and the stars were bright overhead. The weather was perfect. It wasn't too hot or too cool. It was going to be a great night. Elise was looking forward to getting drunk tonight. Walt was planning on having a few, but he didn't want to get too drunk. Someone had to look after Elise. He knew what she could be like when she got really drunk, and it wasn't always pretty.

•　　•　　•

Joshua pulled his car off the road and into the gravel. There was a long line of cars parked alongside the road and more in a clear field, directly in front of where the party was happening. He got out of the car and flipped his hoodie over his head. He reached in the back and grabbed a six pack of beer, had to look the part, didn't want to stand out. It was going to be a good night; he could just feel it.

•　　•　　•

Elise was ready to let her hair down. She met up with Hailey and Ashley and she and Walt went their separate ways, for the time being. He met a couple of friends and they went to smoke a joint. From time to time over the next couple of hours, Walt and Elise would bump into each other. Elise would kiss him quickly and then she would be gone again. The last time he couldn't help but notice that she was starting to get pretty drunk. The next time he saw her, he was going to stay with her, just to make sure that she was safe.

Some time had passed, he hadn't seen her for a while and he started to worry.

"Hey buddy, have you seen Elise?" he asked, grabbing the shoulder of some guy in a blue hoodie.

He meant to turn him, so that he could see his face, but the guy just pulled free from him and kept walking. Not everyone was friendly tonight, he thought, and continued looking for Elise.

He looked around the perimeter of the party, where it was darker. He saw a couple of Abe's buddies standing near the half dozen or so tents that had been set up, so he went to talk to them.

"Hey, have you guys seen Elise?" Walt asked.

"Nope, not for a while," they said.

"Where's Abe tonight, haven't seen him," Walt asked.

"Haven't seen him for a while," Trent said, looking over Walt's shoulder, to the farthest tent at the back.

Walt had a sick feeling in the pit of his stomach, that he got when he feared the worst. He hurried in the direction of the tent.

"You don't want to go over there. It's nothing to do with you. Just turn around and go back to the party, Walt," Trent said.

Walt ignored him and marched toward the tent. He ripped open the zipper and looked inside. Abe had his pants down around his ankles and he couldn't see who was under him, but he could see that she had blonde hair.

"Get the fuck out of here! What the fuck man!" Abe said.

"Walt is that you?" Ashley asked.

"Ashley? Are you okay?"

"I would be, if you'd close the tent and let us get back to what we were doing."

"Oh, sorry. I was looking for Elise."

"Well she's not in here, as you can tell," she said, sarcastically.

Walt closed the tent and turned back toward the party. Chuck and Trent just shrugged their shoulders, as if to say, I told you so.

Walt stood looking across the mass of people, trying to catch a glimpse of Elise. Then he heard her laugh. He would know it anywhere. It was coming from the far-side of the large bonfire, in the middle of the party. He started to snake his way through the crowd of people. He could still hear her laughing and he followed the sound of it. The guy with the blue hoodie was walking in front of him again. Every now and then, he would catch a glimpse of him. Walt thought again, what a dick and then focused again on finding Elise. He rounded the fire and through the mass of bodies, he could see Elise standing near the fire, talking to Hailey. He made a bee-line, straight for her. The guy in the blue hoodie was now out in the open and was nearly to where Elise and Hailey stood, laughing and talking. Elise saw Walt and waved to him smiling and laughing.

"Waaallllltttt!!" she yelled, waving wildly at him.

Walt waved back and continued in her direction.

As the guy in the hoodie approached Elise, he seemed to lose his balance. He stumbled and fell into Elise. He put his arms out to brace himself and they landed on Elise's shoulders. She stumbled backward and disappeared into the large bonfire. It seemed to happen in slow-motion. Walt was too far away to do anything, but watch in horror. He pushed his way through the crowd, to the other side of the fire. He got there, just in time to see Elise emerge from the fire, seemingly unscathed.

"Woohoo!" Elise yelled, in a long holler of triumph, as she emerged from the fire.

Walt was still pushing his way through the crowd to get to her. He couldn't believe that she was alright.

Elise had her arms stretched above her head, hooting and hollering, her head flung back. She took a step forward and it landed on a small log. She lost her balance and fell backward. She disappeared completely into the fire except for her feet.

She started screaming, instantly. This was a different scream. This was a loud, blood-curdling, scream of pain. Walt got to the fire, just as she rolled out of it. He grabbed her by the feet and pulled her away from the fire.

"Call 911!" he screamed, and several kids pulled out their phones and began to dial.

Elise's hair was completely burned off, except for a little tuft, just above her forehead. The back of her head was red and black in spots and others were white. Her clothes were charred and some parts were missing. Where her skin could be seen, it was bright red. Both hands were white and waxy looking and there was some skin hanging off them She was holding them in the air above her. She was lying on her side, in a fetal position and she was crying out in agony. Walt was lying on the ground, facing her, trying to keep her calm. Elise was shaking uncontrollably. Walt thought it was from the pain, but he knew enough to know, that she may be going into shock.

A crowd had gathered, to see what all the commotion was about.

A couple of kids had run to the road, to meet the ambulance when it arrived.

Walt continued to talk to Elise, but she hadn't opened her eyes yet. Her breathing was getting shallower and faster. He tried to get her to breathe slowly, in through her nose and out through her mouth, but she continued breathing quickly.

Someone that was standing close by, put a jacket over her.

"She may be going into shock. Best to keep her warm," he said.

"Hang in there Elise. The ambulance should be on its way. Everything will be okay, you'll see," Walt said.

"Can we clear the way for the ambulance, when they come," Walt said.

"We'll take care of it," Trent said.

He and Chuck started moving people back, making a path through the throng of kids that were trying to get a peek of what was going on.

Walt could hear Trent and Chuck yelling at kids to move back. Mercifully, he could also hear the wail of a siren that meant that the ambulance was nearly there. Luckily town was close, and in a small town like theirs, the paramedics were rarely busy.

"Can you hear that? The ambulance is almost here. I love you, so much," Walt said.

Elise didn't respond. She had stopped screaming, but she was moaning and rocking rhythmically back and forth and still hadn't opened her eyes.

The ambulance drove into the laneway and then right back to where Elise was still lying, where Walt had dragged her.

The ambulance came to a stop and two paramedics jumped from it and attended to Elise immediately.

They asked Walt a battery of questions, that he tried to answer as best as he could. Questions like; how long was it since she had been burned? How long was she in contact with the fire? Had she been drinking? If he knew if she was allergic to any drugs. There were more questions, but Walt wasn't thinking clearly any longer and he wasn't sure what they were asking.

They worked quickly. They poured water on her clothes to try to cool her skin down as much as they could. They wrapped her hands in clean, white bandages and then loaded her on a stretcher and had her in the back of the ambulance in no time.

He'd held it together, for Elise. Now that there was someone there to help her, he broke down. He was a basket case and he barely remembered the trip to the hospital. They didn't want to let him ride in the back of the ambulance, but he wasn't taking no for an answer. Walt sat beside Elise and talked to her. He wanted so much to comfort her, but he didn't know where it was safe to touch her, so he refrained from doing so, altogether.

Becky, the one paramedic, continued to work on Elise. She put a mask on her, to give her oxygen. She said it was in case she breathed in the heat and or smoke from the fire, and damaged her lungs. She also hooked up an I.V. To her arm. She asked Elise several questions and she was able to respond. She still had her eyes closed, but at least she was responding. Walt was glad that her eyes were closed. He was sure, that no matter how hard he tried to hide the horror and shock that he was feeling, that he would fail miserably.

•   •   •

He remembered calling Elise's parents, but he had no idea what he had said to them. When they got to the hospital, they rushed Elise into one of the Emergency rooms and he was asked to stay in the waiting room. Bill and Sharon showed up ten minutes later. They bombarded him with questions. He felt like screaming, but he did his best to answer them all, without losing his cool. After the initial burst of questions, they sat silently, waiting for the doctor to appear.

The doctor came and found them, about an hour later.

"We are going to let you see her briefly. She has suffered second degree and third degree burns to the back of her legs, torso, arms, neck and head. Her hands were burnt the worst. We have her on I.V. and a ventilator and we have covered her burns for now. I'm letting you see her now, because we are going to put her in a medically induced coma for the time being, so that she won't be in pain. The pain associated with these types of burns, can be excruciating. We will be changing her dressings every several hours and we may need to do some skin grafts, in the near future. She is resting comfortably right now. She is heavily sedated, so she may not know you're there, but you can go in and see her now. Then we'll be transferring her to her own room," the doctor said.

He followed us into the room and gave us a brief description of what to expect. He said it was too early to tell, just how bad the damage was, and that they would know more in a couple of days.

Elise was sleeping when they went in to see her. She had a large plastic tube down her throat, an I.V. in her arm and a bunch of monitors hooked up to her. She looked like a mummy. She was nearly covered in white bandages. The only thing that wasn't covered was her face. Walt, Bill and Sharon all took their turn talking to her, kissing her on the cheek and then they left. When they got back to the waiting room, Ashley and Hailey were there. They told them everything that they knew up to that point about Elise's condition and then they left as well.

Walt felt guilty, just leaving her and going home, but there was nothing he could do for her right now. Bill and Sharon gave him a ride home. He had completely forgotten about their bikes, that were still out at the party. He would have to go get them in the morning.

He found it impossible to shut off the thoughts that kept going around in his head, but eventually he fell asleep.

In the morning, Walt walked out to where the party had been the night before. Their bikes were still propped against a tree, where they had left them. He walked past them and into the clearing, where the party had been. There were still a few people sitting by their tents and a couple of kids that had passed out on the lawn. He walked over to where the fire had been blazing, hours before. The blackened logs that remained, were smoldering and a few glowing embers were still visible in the middle. The smell of campfires was always one of his favourite things, until now that was. He hated the smell of it. He spat into the middle of the logs, in a show of disgust. He sat on his haunches, closed his eyes and wept. Why did this have to happen? Why Elise? There was no one, more kind and giving than she was. Why her?

He didn't hear the person approach from behind him.

"How's Elise? Is she okay?" Trent asked.

Walt wiped at his eyes quickly, removing the tears. He cleared his throat, trying to remove the lump in it. He stood up and turned around.

"She's alive. They put her in a medically induced coma for the time being, to help with the pain. We won't know for a few days, just how bad the burns are," Walt said.

"Oh, okay. Well, take care of yourself Walt, and tell her that we're thinking about her, when you get the chance."

"I will, thanks."

Trent turned and went back to his tent and Walt went back toward the road, to where their bikes were. He put Elise's bike across his handle bars and road back home.

He was lost. He couldn't go anywhere without thinking about Elise. He missed her smile, her bubbly personality and the feel of her.

• • •

When he wasn't sitting at school, Walt was at Elise's bedside, talking to her. She had been in a coma for two weeks. There were times that he wasn't permitted to stay. They had to change her bandages frequently and assess her recovery. The doctors didn't know 100%, what her level of recovery would be, but they did have an idea of what to expect and they did their best to prepare Sharon, Bill and Walt. She would never be able to grow hair on most of her head and she was in for a lot of operations and a lot of therapy. Walt knew of one other person that had been burnt badly and it took years before he resumed some semblance of a normal life. He was in pain a lot of the time and his mobility was severely restricted. It pained him to think, that was what Elise had in store for her.

Her hands were badly damaged and she would never regain full use of them. Her one ear was severely burnt and she would have scarring on the one side of her face. She was in for a long road to recovery.

Walt couldn't bear the thought of seeing Elise go through all of that. Right now, she wasn't in pain and that was good, but she would eventually be brought out of her coma. The pain probably wouldn't be as bad by then, but she would still be in pain. There was also the psychological pain that she would have to endure, that worried Walt. She had always been the most beautiful girl in school. How was she going to come to terms with the way she looked now? Only time would tell how bad it would really be, but right now, it didn't look good. Walt thought, that if he could change spots with her, then he would gladly do so.

The doctor and nurse had shooed him from her room. It was nice to get away once in a while, but he felt guilty, all the same. He needed a break, to just relax and not have to worry about Elise and what the future held for the two of them. His favourite place to go was down by the dam, no surprise there. He could sit there and let his troubles wash away with the current of the river. All his troubles were forgotten when he was there and he was free to remember, only the good times that he and Elise shared.

He was sunning himself on a rock. He had his eyes closed and he was enjoying the warmth of the sun and the peacefulness of his surroundings. He wasn't thinking about anything, which was a good thing. His mind needed theses breaks, so that he could recharge and be there for Elise, when she needed him most. She would need the support when she awoke from her coma. He put those thoughts out of his head and continued to enjoy the sun and the sound of the flowing water. This was as content as he had been, in a long time. It had been such a stressful few weeks and he hadn't really understood how much, until this moment. As much as he was enjoying his time here, he had goofed off long enough. He wanted to get back and see Elise. Sharon and Bill should be there by the time he got back and he wanted to see if they had any new news about her condition or when they were going to bring her out of her coma.

He sat up quickly and he had to stay seated until his head-rush subsided. When his head felt right, he got up and headed up the final slope to the road. Joshua was walking toward him, with a brown lunch bag in his hand, whistling as he walked. Walt nodded to him and Joshua nodded back.

"Wonderful day, isn't it?" Joshua said.

"Sure is," Walt said and continued walking.

"I come here most days, to eat my lunch. It's a good place to relax and unwind."

Walt didn't want to be rude, but he needed to get going. He didn't have time for idle chit chat.

"Yep," Walt said, and continued walking.

Joshua sat down on a rock and began to eat his lunch. It was good to see Walt again, he thought. He would almost say that he had missed him. Things had taken a little longer than he had expected, with his last job, but he was glad to be back here. This would have been a good spot to call home, if he would have had the opportunity. For now, he would just have to be happy with being here for the short time that it would take to deal with Walt and Elise. He had never had a case that had played itself out as many times as these two. He figured it must have been the strength of the love that they shared, that had him coming back again and again. Then he thought that maybe, just maybe, it was because he liked coming here. He liked the town and he liked Elise and Walt, and the more times he could get them to start over, the more times he was needed. Whatever it was, he was just happy to be back, sitting on this rock and eating his lunch.

There was something familiar about that guy, Walt thought, dismissed it and continued walking, back to the hospital.

A couple of days later, they got the news that they were going to bring Elise out of her coma. The doctor warned them, that she was still going to be in a lot of pain, but that they would give her something to control it. Walt's biggest concern at this point, was how Elise was going to take the news of her condition. The hair on most of her head would never grow back and her hands were never going to be very useful to her.

Elise was disoriented for quite a while when she woke up. She didn't know why she was in the hospital and she didn't remember being burned. She wanted to see a mirror. They tried to talk her out of it, but she demanded to have a mirror brought to her.

Sharon gave her a small mirror from her purse. Elise tried to hold it up to see, but couldn't. Sharon held it for her and she stared into it for the longest time. Tears began to roll down her cheeks.

"How bad is it?" she asked.

"Don't worry about that now. You just woke up. Try to relax and concentrate on getting better," Sharon said.

"How bad?" Elise said, as loud as she could muster.

"It's bad sweetheart, but you're alive and you are surrounded by a lot of people that love you," Sharon said, crying.

"Can you just leave me for a bit," Elise said.

"Oh honey, we're here for you," Sharon said.

"I just want to be left alone for a bit! Is that okay?" she yelled and broke into tears.

Walt, Bill and Sharon, kissed her on the cheek and went down the hall, to a small sitting area. Sharon was in tears and Bill was doing his best to console her. Walt sat staring at the wall. He was numb. He didn't know how to feel, what to think. He felt like his heart was about to break, he felt so bad for Elise. He just wanted her to know that he loved her so much, no matter what. He would do anything for her.

Shortly after, the nurses went in to change her dressings and Walt could hear her screaming from down the hall. He covered his ears with his hands, to no avail. He felt guilty as Hell, but he had to get out of there and clear his head.

He ran out of the hospital and didn't stop until he got to the river.

The older gentleman that he had seen eating his lunch, the other day, was there again. Great, he's going to want to talk again, Walt thought. He was in no mood for conversation. He just wanted to be left alone.

Joshua got up from where he was sitting and came over to where Walt was standing, looking at the river.

"If you don't mind me saying, you look like a man that's down on his luck. I don't mean to be presumptuous, but I think I can help. The name's Joshua," he said, extending his hand.

Walt reluctantly held out his hand, to shake Joshua's. A blue spark shot from his fingertips to Walt's. Walt laughed a bit, in spite of himself.

"Hi, I'm Walt," he said, shaking Joshua's hand up and down.

Walt stood looking into Joshua's eyes. All his troubles seemed to melt away, and in that moment, he knew, that everything was going to be alright.

"I know that things can seem overwhelming at times, but I'm here to tell you, that every problem, no matter how daunting it may seem, can be solved. Why don't you come by my place later tonight and we can talk about it a little more? Say, nine o'clock, 23 Maple street?"

"Okay" Walt said dreamily, and then walked off in the direction of home.

Chapter Twenty

Walt went home and laid down for a nap. He was exhausted for some reason and he completely forgot about going back to the hospital to see Elise. All he could think about right now, was getting home and crawling into bed. He slipped between his sheets without even removing his clothes and as soon as his head hit his pillow he was out.

He was sitting in a back alley. He had long hair and tattoos and he felt miserable, and he had had this dream before. A slender black man was holding out a gun for him to take. He reached for it and a bright blue spark jumped across the darkness of the alley. The spark went into his hand and ran up his arm. It tickled and he shivered a bit at the feel of it. He looked down at the gun that was now in his hand. He looked up at the man. It was Joshua that he had met earlier in the day, down by the river. Joshua smiled at him and he felt warm inside, content. He breathed in deeply and let it out. All his troubles seemed to wash away. Walt smiled back at Joshua, lifted the gun to his temple and squeezed the trigger.

Walt sat up in his bed, his heart racing. He looked around the room and realized that it had just been a dream. He lie back down and closed his eyes. It took a few minutes for his heart rate and his breathing to return to normal and then he fell back to sleep again.

He was standing in the middle of a gravel parking lot, just like the dream he had had many times, over the years. He looked around and noticed that it wasn't a parking lot after all. It was a quarry, and he was standing in the middle of it. He heard a gunshot and he spun in its direction. Another shot rang out from the other side of the quarry.

It was dark, and Walt could see the flames shooting out of the barrel of the gun. He walked in its direction.

He found Joshua, setting a tin can atop a wooden frame. There were shards of broken glass everywhere beneath his feet. Joshua held the gun out to him and he took it. A blue spark ran up his hand. He smiled and stroked the handle of the gun. He raised it and shot. One of the tin cans went cartwheeling backwards into the darkness. He raised it and shot again. The other can went careening wildly off to his left. He smiled an impossibly large smile and looked over at Joshua, who was smiling back at him.

"There's still one more in the chamber. I'll see you on the other side," Joshua said, and made a tipping gesture to an imaginary hat on his head.

Walt put the gun to his temple and squeezed the trigger.

He awoke from his dream. He was sweating and his heart was beating like a jack hammer. He threw back the covers and went to his window and opened it, letting in some fresh air. He breathed in the cool air and removed his t-shirt. It felt wonderful against his hot, clammy stomach. He stood that way for a while, until he had cooled himself sufficiently, then went back to bed.

He lie on his bed, with the covers peeled back, staring at the ceiling. He knew that he should get moving, go back to the hospital, but he was busy thinking about the dreams that he had.

It didn't make any sense. He had been having variations of the same dream, for as long as he could remember and now they had been taken to a whole other level. He supposed it was probably just the stress that he was under, playing tricks with his mind. What else could it be. It was probably just because he had seen Joshua at the dam earlier, just his mind's way of dealing with it. Speaking of that; he had better get back to the hospital, to see Elise.

When he got there, Sharon and Bill had left for the day, and so, he had Elise all to himself. Elise was lying there watching the T.V. when he arrived.

"Hey," she said.

"Hey yourself. How you are you feeling?" Walt asked.

"Honestly? I wish I would have died in that fire. I know that's a terrible thing for me to say, but I think it would have been better for everyone. The doctor was here and gave me the full run down of my condition. It's going to take months and I'm still going to be a freak, after everything is said and done. It's not fair to my parents and it isn't fair to you," she said and started to cry.

Walt wiped the tears from her cheeks, with his fingers, but there were more tears to replace them with. He went to her side table and got a box of tissues to wipe them away, as they appeared.

"You shouldn't think like that. Your parents and I love you very much. We would do anything for you. Don't worry about us, we'll be just fine. Concentrate on getting better."

"Yeah, you'll be just fine, but I won't. From what the doctor said, I'll be lucky if my hands ever work right again. Most of my hair isn't going to grow back and the back of me is all melted. My one ear is mostly gone and the one side of my face is melted as well. I made him show it to me, when they changed my bandages. I stand by what I said earlier. I would have been better off; we all would have been better off, if I would have just died in that fire," she said, breaking into tears again.

Walt wiped the tears from her face and then kissed her on the lips. At least the tube had been removed from her throat, so that he could do that much. He was afraid to touch her anywhere else, for fear of hurting her.

"I love you. You. I don't love you because you are the most beautiful girl in school. I love you because you are the most beautiful girl I know, inside. I know it won't be easy, especially for you, but I also know that you're a fighter and that you won't give up. Your parents and I will be here, every step of the way. I for one, am so happy you didn't die in that fire. I can't imagine a life without you in it. That would be the only time that I would want to give up on living. As long as we have each other, everything else, we'll figure it out."

"I know you're right. I just need time to have my pity party. You guys have had weeks to come to terms with this. I've only just begun to process this. Don't you ever wish that you could go back and do things over. I mean, if I would have stayed with you, or if I hadn't drunk so much, or if I hadn't gone to the party at all, none of this would have happened."

"I've had lots of times, that I wished that I could have gone back and done things over. That's why they say that hindsight is twenty-twenty. We can't live our lives thinking, what if? We just have to do the best that we can, with what we have. I'm devastated by what happened to you, but I do know one thing. I can handle anything that life throws at us, as long as we're together."

"You sound like one big cliché," she said, trying to laugh a little.

"I know you're right. Maybe I'll be able to see some positives, later. Right now, it's hard, you know?"

"I get it. I can only imagine what you are going through."

"Thanks for being here. I love you, Walt."

"I love you, too. There's no place else that I would be right now."

"Well, you could go home. I love seeing you, but I'm so tired. I need to sleep. I hope you understand."

"No, of course. Yeah, you should get some rest. I'll be back in the morning."

"Come here, before you go."

Walt leaned forward and kissed her and held the side of her face with his right hand. It felt wonderful to kiss her again. At that moment, all their troubles were forgotten. All he could think of, was how happy he was that she hadn't died in that fire. Maybe he was being selfish, but he wanted her here, beside him, forever.

"That was nice. I'll see you in the morning?"

"I'll be here," Walt said.

She seemed to be feeling better and that made him happy. He walked home, thinking of her as he went. No matter what, he was glad that she hadn't died in that fire. If he could go back and change things he would, but God knows that wasn't possible, so they had to do the best with what they were given.

Walt went home and ate some leftovers that G-ma had left in the refrigerator for him. He looked at the clock on the wall above the kitchen table. It was ten after six. He had a lot of time to kill before he was going to meet Joshua. Why was he going to meet Joshua? It seemed like a good idea at the time, but for the life of him, he couldn't remember why. What could he possibly say or do, that would change the situation? He hoped that he wasn't a drug dealer or something. No, he got the feeling that that wasn't it.

Walt thought of the dreams that he had had earlier. Strange. Oddly realistic. They felt more real, more tangible than a normal dream. They felt almost like memories, somehow.

His impending meeting with Joshua intrigued him. It had more to do with his dreams he thought, but it would still be interesting to see what he had to say, nevertheless. He didn't know the guy, but he liked him all the same. It was probably just a case of an old man wanting some company and wanting someone to talk to. He could use the company right now as well. What could it hurt?

He went to his room and picked one of the many pictures of Elise from his dresser. It was the one that her Mom had taken of her in her cheerleading uniform. She was smiling happily and holding her one leg up over head. Breathtakingly beautiful. Walt had known her for his entire life and only he knew that she was as beautiful on the inside as she was on the outside, maybe even more so. He would love her no matter what. He wasn't in love with her looks. He didn't feel sorry for himself. Oh no, he wouldn't have a hot girlfriend anymore; that was certainly not it. He felt bad for her; even though he knew that looks weren't everything to Elise either. He just wished that she didn't have to go through what she was going through. It would be a long painful road and he wished that he could spare her that. That's all.

He set the picture back down on his dresser and laid on his bed. He continued to think of Elise, but the dreams that he had had were still forcing their way in. Normally, he would forget his dreams shortly after waking up. These were different. They weren't fading, if anything, they were getting more vivid.

He turned on the T.V. to try and distract himself and for the time-being, it worked. He watched a couple of mindless shows of some idiots nearly killing themselves doing stupid things, until it was time for him to go.

If he walked slowly enough, he would get to Joshua's place around nine. He threw on a light pullover jacket and headed for the door.

"Going somewhere?" G-ma asked.

"Yeah. Just have to see a friend for a minute. Won't be long."

"Okay dear."

Walt walked slowly toward the other end of town and toward Maple street. He still wasn't entirely sure why he was going and he had no idea what this Joshua would want to talk to him about. He had certainly piqued his interest though and he would find out soon enough.

Walt turned onto Maple street and walked past a couple of houses, before he saw a couple of the numbers out front. He was at 76 Maple, so he crossed the road. He was sure that Joshua had said 25 Maple, and that would be on the other side of the road.

He got close to the house, but he didn't see any lights on.

"Good evening," he heard from the porch of the next house. He recognized Joshua's voice at once.

"Hey. How's it going?" Walt said, walking up the drive to where Joshua was sitting, smoking his pipe.

"So? What brings you by?" Joshua asked, taking a long haul on his pipe and letting it out slowly.

The fragrance from his pipe was everywhere. Walt decided that he liked the smell of it. He liked it very much.

"What? I came by because you asked me to," Walt said, puzzled.

"Sure, but what brings you by? Are you in the habit of accepting invitations from people that you have never met?"

"No... listen, I could leave, if that's what you want."

"Is that what you want?" Joshua asked, leaning forward in his chair and looking at Walt, intently.

"I don't know what I want. It doesn't matter what I want. It's not like I can change anything, anyway," Walt blurted.

"Okay. So now we're getting somewhere. You say that you don't know what you want, but Ahh, I think you do. You say that you couldn't change it anyway. What if you could?"

"What if I could, what?"

"Change what ever it is that has you troubled; whatever it is that you would change, if you could?" Joshua said, his eyes twinkling mischievously.

Walt had a feeling that he was just toying with him now and he wasn't sure that he liked it. He wasn't sure, just exactly what his angle was.

"Okay. I can see that you're losing patience with me. I'm going to level with you. What would you say, if I told you that I could help you? What would you say, if I told you that I could help both you and Elise?" Joshua said, still sitting forward in his seat.

"How could you do that? Are you a doctor, or homeopathic healer or something?"

"Oh. I'm something. Never mind that. Answer the question. If there was a way for you to help Elise, would you?"

"Of course I would. I would do anything for Elise. I would die for her!" Walt said defiantly.

"Good answer. Right answer," Joshua said, and continued to puff on his pipe.

When he had finished his pipe, he knocked out the ashes with the palm of his hand and stuffed it in his pocket.

"Come on in. We need to talk and I don't want the neighbours eavesdropping."

Once in side, Joshua began to speak again. Walt was looking at the hutch that was across from him, as he sat at the table. It looked very familiar to him.

"I can help you, both of you. I'm going to tell you a story. It might seem a little unbelievable at first, but hear it through to the end and then you can decide where we go from there. Does that sound fair?" Joshua said.

"Sounds fair. I'm all ears. Tell me why you've invited me here tonight. I'm very interested in what you have to say," Walt said.

Joshua had told his story countless times over the years, but he never grew tired of telling it. He enjoyed how engaged his audience was. It was always the same. He could see them yearning for more, hanging on his every word.

"I was born in the south. My parents were slaves and so upon birth, I was also a slave," Joshua started, but Walt stopped him.

"Let me stop you right there. Unless you're well over a hundred years old or my math is completely wrong, then you're either a liar or you're just telling a story," Walt said.

"Okay, okay. I don't need to go back that far anyway. I'll give you as true an account as I can recall."

"My early years were a struggle but when I got older I thought that I was really living the life. I was living in a nice house, I had a nice car and I was making lots of money. I had moved to Boston and I became an accountant. I was doing the books of some very influential people. I thought that I had made it. I couldn't have been further from the truth. They owned me. It was as though I were a slave."

"Now I understand the reference to being a slave," Walt interjected. "Sorry, please continue."

"I tried to believe that I was happy. How could I not be? I had everything that I wanted. Ahh, but I didn't have anything. Some very old clichés are there because they are so true. Money can't buy happiness is one of them. I had to jump when my clients said to and I had to work long hours sometimes when I didn't want to. My life was not my own. Sure, I had a lot of money, but I didn't have the time to enjoy it or someone to enjoy it with.

When I first moved to Boston I met a beautiful girl name Maggie. She was white and had long blonde hair. Well, back then, a white girl dating a black man was not an everyday occurrence and it certainly wasn't accepted. We didn't give a hoot what anyone thought. We were in love and that was all that mattered. That should have been enough, but I had to prove to her and to me that they were all wrong. I had to prove that I deserved to be with Maggie. She couldn't care a less about a fancy car or a fancy house, but I was determined to give her the best of everything. All she wanted was me, but I was too stupid to see it. I worked long hours and spent less and less time with her. I kept chasing something that wasn't there. What I should have realized, was that what I truly wanted was right in front of me.

What's that expression? You don't know what you have 'til it's gone. Well, one day I came home from another long night at the office. I was exhausted and all I wanted to do was curl up on the sofa with Maggie and have a glass of wine and talk. The sofa was gone and so was Maggie. I tried to contact her but she wouldn't return my calls. She went to stay with her sister. I tried to talk to her there but her sister called the cops on me. I tried a couple more times over the next few weeks but she wouldn't talk to me. Now I could see what I couldn't, when Maggie was still around. She was the most important thing in my life and without her, nothing else mattered. I wrote her countless letters, apologizing for my behaviour and begging for her to forgive me. She never responded but the silence spoke volumes. She had moved on. Everything would have been okay I guess, if my eyes hadn't been opened to the fact that there is more to life than money. I could have been completely content to work like a madman and I would have become extremely wealthy. But, my eyes were now fully open; now that it was too late. I became extremely depressed. I couldn't hardly think let alone work. If I did think it was only about Maggie and how much I had screwed up. I wanted to kill myself but I was too much of a coward to do it. So, I did it slowly. I had lots of money at my disposal and I was no longer saving for a rainy day, so the sky was the limit. Suddenly, I had all kinds of new friends to party with and all sorts of beautiful women to sleep with. I spent seventy thousand dollars in five months and I was more miserable than when I started. I continued to drink and do drugs. My clients had dropped me long ago and so I had no new money coming in. Every time I thought that I had hit rock bottom, the bottom was pulled out from beneath me and I went tumbling further down into an abyss that I had no way of pulling myself free of.

It was Christmas morning and I sat in front of an undecorated tree in my living room. There were no presents under it, no parties to attend and no loved ones. I had finally and completely hit rock bottom and I no longer wanted to crawl out of the hole that I was in. All I wanted, was for it to end. I went to the bedroom, got my thirty-eight from my sock drawer, carried it out into the living room and sat down on the sofa. I didn't spend hours contemplating where I went wrong, or thinking of reasons why I should live. I lifted the gun, put the barrel against my temple and pulled the trigger."

Walt sat for a while mulling over what he had just heard. It seemed to him that Joshua was telling a tall tale. He had heard this story before, he was nearly positive. It could have been in one of the books that Elise had read to him. He couldn't remember reading the book himself, so that had to be it. Anyway, it didn't much matter. What he really wanted to know, was why he had bothered to tell him the story at all.

"Okay? I'm confused. Why did you bother to tell me that story and what does that have to do with either Elise or me?" Walt asked.

"I'm sensing that you don't believe me," he said, turning his head and pointing to the scar on his left temple and then turning and pointing to the scars on his right temple.

"You got that right."

Joshua didn't know what to think. This all hinged on him believing his story. They always did and they always decided to go back and live their miserable lives again. Hell, Walt had on two occasions already. He was caught off guard a little. He hadn't foreseen this being a problem. He needed a moment to regroup and think of his next move.

"You want something to drink?" he asked.

"Sure."

Joshua went to the refrigerator and came back with two beers. He handed one to Walt and a familiar blue spark jumped from his hand to Walt's. Maybe now he'll be more co-operative, Joshua thought.

Walt seemed unaffected. He seemed like he hardly noticed. Where to go from here? This is where he usually went on to offer them a chance to go back and do it all again, and they were usually eager to do it. He hadn't gotten that far. What to do? He took another swig of his beer and let out a long exhale, trying to gather himself.

"Okay. I'm in the people business, Walt. I'm going to level with you. We've met before. What I'm about to say is going to sound crazy, but it's the truth. I can offer you a chance to go back and live your life again. You can go back to a time before your parents died, back to a time before Elise had her accident. I can offer you a second chance, a fresh start. How does that sound?"

"I would say, that if that were true, then I'd be all in. What do you mean that we've met before?"

"We've had this conversation before. I gave you a second chance before and you took it. This is not your first time 'round."

Walt sat, looking at him without blinking. Joshua could tell that he was starting to get to him. One last piece to the puzzle. The revolver should be able to talk him into believing the rest of the story.

Joshua got up and opened the top drawer of the hutch and removed a small box. He set the box on the table and spun it, so that the latch was facing Walt.

"Go ahead. Open it."

Walt flicked the latch open and lifted the lid. Inside was the revolver, resting on its crushed velvet cushion.

"Go ahead pick it up," Joshua said.

He had to cover his mouth to hide his huge smile. He knew that once he touched the gun, it would be all over for him. She had a way of getting into your soul, making you want to be with her more than anything.

Walt reached for the gun and a blue spark jumped from the gun and spread out across Walt's hand. Walt was turning the gun over in his hands, a dull, vacant, expressionless look on his face. Joshua smiled widely again, but Walt didn't notice.

"Let's go for a walk and I'll finish my story while we do," Joshua said, and then got up from the table.

"You go ahead and keep that until we get where we're going."

"Okay," Walt said dreamily.

Walt followed him out the back of the house, down a little dirt trail and out into the gravel pit. The sky was clear and the stars shone brightly overhead. It was quite light out, considering it was now nearly eleven o'clock. Walt could see the wood frame with a couple of tin cans set atop it, along with a whiskey bottle. There were shards of glass everywhere. It reminded him of his dream.

Joshua had been talking the whole time that they had been walking, but he barely heard a word that he was saying. He was so focused on the gun in his hand, that nothing else mattered.

"So? Are you ready for this?" Joshua asked.

"I'm ready,"

"I'll see you on the other side," Joshua said.

Joshua took the gun from him, loaded it and then handed it back to him and then took a couple of steps back.

Walt took it from him, and immediately lifted the gun and pulled the trigger.

He slumped to the floor of the gravel pit. His lifeless eyes staring up at the millions of bright stars overhead.

He took a couple of steps forward, bent down and placed his hand on his shoulder. He took the gun, then removed his pipe from his pocket and started to walk back in the direction of his house. Behind him, all evidence of the lifeless body that had been there a moment before, was gone. He lit his pipe as he walked.

"Another night, another job well done. A new beginning," he said to the still night, and began whistling happily.

CHAPTER TWENTY-ONE

The next morning, Walt never showed up at the hospital. Elise thought that maybe he had slept in. She knew that he had been under a lot of stress since all this had happened. She hadn't really thought about it much, until now. She was too busy dealing with it herself. When lunch time came and he still hadn't showed up, she began to worry. Her Mom was supposed to pop in for a few minutes during her lunch hour. She would wait and ask her if she'd seen him, before she started to panic.

Sharon showed up at 12:30, and she was alone. She hadn't seen Walt, but she said that she would swing by his house on the way to the hospital this afternoon. That would be five hours from now. That was a long time, when all you had to do was think. She had the T.V. to watch, but she hated daytime T.V. Nothing to watch but game shows, talk shows and soap operas. She hated reality shows, but even they would be welcome viewing, after watching weeks of daytime television.

Reading would definitely help, but she couldn't use her hands well enough to hold a book. Her Mom was supposed to get her an e-reader, but that probably wouldn't be until the weekend, when she had more time.

Elise was making good progress. Her hands were in bad shape and they would need physiotherapy, but the doctor thought that she would have at least partial use of them, when everything was said and done. Her hair was starting to grow back, although it was very patchy, so she would need to wear a wig. Her ear would need some cosmetic surgery, as well as the side of her face and she would need several surgeries on the scarring on the back of her legs and back. All in all, it was better than they had originally feared. She was scheduled to be released from the hospital in the next week or so. She couldn't wait. She would feel more comfortable at home, sleeping in her own bed. Walt could come whenever he wanted and stay as long as he wanted. Walt, where was he? She began to worry again. It wasn't like him to be late, and it certainly wasn't like him to not show up at all.

• • •

Joshua decided that under the circumstances, that he should probably lie low for a while, at least until Elise was out of the hospital. He jumped into his car and drove to the next town over. He didn't want to get too far away, just far enough that he wouldn't be recognized by anyone. He wanted to be able to get back there quickly, when he knew that Elise was out of the hospital, out and about, and on her own.

He would miss Walt, he thought. Oh well, he still had Elise. He was anxious to see her. He hadn't seen her since the accident, and he found that he missed her. What a sentimental old fool. He wasn't that old after all. Besides, you're only as old as you feel, and right now, he felt like he was nineteen again.

He rolled down the window, breathed in the fresh air and began to whistle. It was most certainly a good day to be alive.

• • •

Sharon came to the hospital at 5:30, but still no Walt. She had stopped by his house, but he wasn't there.

"I knocked loudly on the front door and then I went to the back door, to do the same. No answer. His Grandma never answered either, but she may have been napping. I'm not sure. Strange. I wonder where he got to?"

"I'm scared Mom. Something must have happened to him. It's not like him, to just not show up. If he had something going on, he would

179

have told me or told you or Dad. Something is definitely up! Can you please check again when you go home? Call me to let me know what you find out."

"I will honey, I promise."

Elise visited with her Mom for a while but she was distracted and couldn't concentrate. Sharon had to keep repeating herself over and over.

"I'm just going to go now and check on Walt. It's obvious that you're too worried about him, to visit with me."

"I'm sorry. Would you mind?" Elise asked.

"Of course not, honey. I'll let you know as soon as I find out something We'll talk soon."

"Thanks Mom. Love you."

"Love you too, sweetheart."

• • •

Joshua settled into a small room, in an old but clean little hotel on the edge of town. It was mostly empty at the moment, except for one trucker who was staying in the room on the end. Joshua went into his room to lie down. Normally he liked to have an afternoon nap. He was usually up quite late. That's when most of his work was done. He would find people that had just left the bar after last call. It was his experience, that most people that were out late and alone, were some of the unhappiest people around. These were the people that were more apt to want a fresh start, a chance for redemption or salvation, or whatever it was that they thought that he was offering them.

Joshua lie on the bed staring at the ceiling. He was surprisingly, not tired at all. He felt more alive than he had felt in many years. All the small aches and pains that he lived with on a daily basis, seemed to be gone. He felt great and he had Walt to thank for that.

• • •

Sharon called Elise's room. Elise clumsily grabbed the phone from its receiver with both hands and held it to her good ear.

"I'm sorry honey. No one has seen him. I talked to his Grandma and she hasn't seen him either. She's beside herself with worry. She wants to file a missing person's report, but I thought that we should come there first. We can call some of his friends and see if they know where he is."

"Yeah, I should have most of their numbers on my cell."

"Okay, we're on our way."

Elise could hear the worry in her Mom's voice as well. Anyone that knew Walt, knew that he would never ditch his G-ma or her, without checking in first. Hopefully he was just with one of his friends and was out of cell phone range or something. They lived in a sleepy little town. Nothing bad ever happened here. Hopefully they would look back in a few hours and laugh at how paranoid they had been.

Sharon and Walt's G-ma were at the hospital a few minutes later. Elise told her Mom who to look for on her cell phone and then she would dial the number and hold the phone out to Elise. They repeated the process, until every one of Walt's friends had been contacted. Nothing. No one had heard from him in days. They were the last people to have seen him, as far as they could tell.

"We're going to the police station, to file a report. I'll let you know as soon as we hear anything," Sharon said.

"I'm coming with you," Elise said attempting to get out of bed.

A fresh stab of pain shot through her hand and she was unable to move her one leg, from the excruciating pain. She fell back in her bed and began to cry.

"We'll keep you updated regularly. I'm sure he's fine. We're probably just over reacting."

Elise wanted to go so badly, but she had to face the fact, that she wasn't ready to leave her bed just yet, let alone go in search of Walt. She had to rely on them. She trusted them, that wasn't it. She just felt helpless lying here and every second that ticked by, would seem like an eternity. She wouldn't be able to relax until Walt was safe and sound.

Walt had seemed completely normal when he left last night. He said that he would see her in the morning and she had every reason to believe that she would. Now he was gone without a trace? It didn't make sense.

Sharon and Walt's Grandma came up empty. His Grandma gave them a picture and they sent it out to the local patrol cars, as well as neighbouring police stations. Then they waited. What else could they do? They had no leads.

Sharon took his Grandma back to the house and they looked in his room for any clues, but they came up empty there as well. His bike was still leaning against the front porch.

"I just remembered something. I was dozing off watching T.V. last night. Walt said he was going to meet a friend for a minute and that he wouldn't be long. I don't understand. You said that you contacted all of his friends," G-ma said.

"Has he had any knew friends over recently?" Sharon asked.

"No. Any free time he has, he spends at the hospital. I haven't seen any of his friends, since before Elise's accident."

"Okay, well it's something, at least. You stay here, in case he comes home. I'm going to tell the police what you told me and then call Elise and see if she knows anything. Here's my cell number, call me if he comes home, or if you remember anything else," Sharon said.

Sharon was really worried at this point as well. Walt was like a son to her. He had been around since he was a toddler and even more since his parents had died. She had to find him. Elise had enough to deal with right now. She didn't need to deal with this as well.

•   •   •

Joshua was full of energy. He couldn't remember ever feeling this good. He supposed that he probably did at one time, but that would have been long ago, and he certainly didn't remember it. He couldn't sit still, he was too fidgety just sitting here doing nothing. He needed to go for a walk. On second thought, no. What he needed to do, was go for a jog. He didn't exactly have any clothes that would pass for jogging attire though. He would have to go into town and buy some.

He drove the short drive into town and stopped at the first store that he came to, that looked like it would have what he needed. It happened to be a thrift store. He found what he wanted quickly and left. He wasn't too concerned by colour or style, as long as they fit.

Before he knew it, he was jogging down a country road. The wind was whistling by as he ran, and he felt more alive than ever. He would have been whistling as he liked to do when he went for walks, but he was smiling too much to do so. He ran around the concession and back to his room. He had a shower, dried off, got dressed and sat out front and smoked his pipe. He wasn't tired or sore in the least. It was a great day to be alive.

•   •   •

Days went by and still no Walt. There were flyers everywhere, with his picture on it. There were no leads, only questions. Days turned into weeks. Elise was released from the hospital and that should have been a joyous occasion. She went to her appointments at the hospital every day and her physiotherapy three times a week. She was already showing vast signs of improvement. She wore special gloves on her hands, and even they had improved, much better than they had hoped for. She wasn't able to return to school yet, but she was able to walk short distances.

She convinced her Mom to take her down to the dam. She wanted to sit by the river for a while. The river soothed her, washed her troubles away.

"Is it alright if you just leave me here for a while. I'd like to be alone for a bit, if that's alright," Elise said.

"Whatever you want, honey. I'll be back in an hour or so, to pick you up."

Normally the sound of the current washing over the rocks, would carry her troubles away. All she could think of was Walt. He had vanished without a trace. At times, she thought that something had happened to him. Other times she would think that he had run away, because he didn't want to deal with his burnt girlfriend. Still other times, she just wished that she could know the truth. Where he was, if he was okay, or if something had indeed happened to him. The worst part was not knowing. She would see him here by the river. She would see him downtown, going around a corner. She would see him in a car passing by on the road. She could hear him call to her from the other side of the river. She would talk to him and make love to him, in her dreams. She could deal with her burns. They turned out to be better than she had hoped and were still improving. What she couldn't deal with, was a life without Walt. She was so lonely. He had always been there. It felt like half of her was missing and she had no idea of how to go on without him.

She got up and made her way gingerly across the bridge and into the clearing on the other side of the river, where she and Walt had made their tree fort when they were kids.

She leaned against the base of the tree. She closed her eyes and remembered back to the day that they had finished it. That was the first time that they had kissed. An awkward, clumsy kiss, but their first kiss nonetheless. She let herself slide down the trunk of the tree until she was sitting in the grass at the base of it. She still had her eyes closed and she was smiling at those memories.

She heard Walt call her name. She opened her eyes and looked around wildly. Her heart was beating faster. She was sure that she had heard him calling to her, but every time that it happened, she was sure that it was him.

She took a deep breath and let it out, trying to calm herself. She closed her eyes again and tried to think of that day, when they had built the fort.

"Elise."

She opened her eyes and struggled to her feet. This time, she was certain that she had heard his voice. She looked around, in all directions, but nothing. Maybe she was losing her mind.

"Elise."

There it was again. It sounded close.

"Elise."

She looked up the ladder to the hole in the floor of the tree house. The trap door was open and there was a dark hole that she couldn't see into. She covered her eyes with her hand and strained to see into the darkness. She had nearly given up and turned away, when Walt stuck his head down through the opening and smiled at her.

"Hey," he said.

She thought that she was dreaming.

Walt grabbed the top rung of the ladder and swung down, landing beside her.

She was overcome with joy. She grabbed him and hugged him, crying all the while. Blue sparks ran up her hands, across her back and disappeared into the air.

"Where have you been? I missed you so much. Why haven't you been here? Where did you go? Why did you go? I don't understand, why you would just leave," she said, crying as she spoke.

When she had finished crying, she pulled back from him, so that she could see him better, and so he could answer her questions.

She stood looking at him with wide eyes and disbelief. She closed her eyes and re-opened them, thinking that it would help. She heard Walt's voice. She would know his voice anywhere. She saw Walt swing out of the tree. She knew it was him. She knew the smell of him. She knew how he felt in her arms. It was Walt. She knew it was. Now when she opened her eyes, there was a slender black man, standing in front of her, wearing a dark pin-striped suit.

"I don't understand. I must be losing my mind. I'm so sorry. I thought that you were somebody else," she said and slumped to the ground, covered her face and began to cry.

"There, there, everything is going to be fine, you'll see. My name is Joshua. I'm in the people business and I'm here to help, and if you don't mind me saying. You look like someone who is down on their luck."

THE END

Walt thought about the dreams that he had and how real they were. Joshua had said that they had met before. Yes, that's right. He did remember meeting him before. That night in the alley. That night in the quarry.

He followed him down the little path and out into the quarry. Joshua was speaking the entire time, but Walt wasn't listening. He was too busy trying to process all the thoughts that were going through his mind. They came back in a flood of memories. He remembered everything. He remembered going to jail. He remembered Elise going to jail. He remembered Elise being raped and he remembered her killing Abe. Most of all, he remembered that Joshua was there for all of it. Yes, they had met before.

Joshua took the gun from him, loaded it and handed it back. Without hesitation Walt lifted the gun and pulled the trigger. The bullet ripped through Joshua's forehead and his lifeless body fell to the floor of the quarry. Blue sparks jumped everywhere. Walt tried to pull away, but before he could, they were on top of him, covering him.

• • •

Joshua looked back to where his body lie on the quarry floor. He reached out to touch his shoulder with his right hand. It was a hand that looked foreign to him; so young, so white.

"Good bye old friend," he said, breathing deeply, filling his lungs with the cool night air.

"It's a good night to be alive."

ALSO BY
DAN MAYER

Twenty-year-old Billy Johnson is afflicted by the hollowness.

All reason is lost when it has him in its grip, pushing him towards acts of unspeakable cruelty. When a hiking accident leaves him injured on an isolated mountain, facing imminent death, Billy looks for meaning in his tragic life. The hollowness, a malevolent force that consumes him, is responsible for the loss of everything good in his life: a relationship with his father, his beloved younger brother Henry, and the first woman to love him, Lisa.

At the peak of despair, on the cusp of death, he encounters a strange old man, who is eerily familiar. Is this Billy's last chance to redeem his troubled life and rid himself of the hollowness?

Thank you so much for reading one of our **Psychological Thrillers**.
If you enjoyed our book, please check out our recommended title for your
next great read!

The Tracker by John Hunt

"A dark thriller that draws the reader in." *–Morning Bulletin*

"I never want to hear mention of bolt-cutters, a live rat and a bucket in the
same sentence again. EVER." *–Ginger Nuts of Horror*

www.ingramcontent.com/pod-product-compliance
Lightning Source LLC
Chambersburg PA
CBHW010448100726
47904CB00008B/2523